Purnell's Book of
ESCAPE
Stories

"He resumed his efforts with the mallet."

Purnell's Book of
ESCAPE
Stories

Purnell

The Publishers would like to thank the following for kindly granting them permission to reproduce the copyrighted extracts and stories included in this anthology: The author, Mr Robert de la Croix, for *Trapped in a Floating Tomb*
Thomas Nelson and Sons Ltd for "From Pretoria to the Sea" from *A Book of Escapes and Hurried Journeys* by John Buchan.

The Compilers have made every effort to clear copyrights and trust that their apologies will be accepted for any errors or omissions.

ISBN 0 361 06693 7
Copyright © 1985 Purnell Publishers Limited.
Published 1985 by Purnell Books, Paulton,
Bristol BS18 5LQ, a member of the BPCC group.
Stories collected by Oyster Books Limited,
Weare, Somerset.
Made and printed in Germany.

British Library Cataloguing in Publication Data

Purnell's book of escape stories.—(Adventure
  stories series)
  1. Children's stories, English
  2. Escapes—Fiction
  I. Rothero, Chris   II. Series
  823′.01′08358   PZ5

ISBN 0-361-06693-7

Contents

The Man in the Bell

by W. E. AYTOUN

In my younger days bell-ringing was much more in fashion among the young men of .... than it is now. Nobody, I believe, practises in there at present except the servants of the church, and the melody has been much injured in consequence. Some fifty years ago, about twenty of us who dwelt in the vicinity of the cathedral formed a club, which used to ring every peal that was called for; and from continual practice and a rivalry which arose between us and a club attached to another steeple, and which tended considerably to sharpen our zeal, we became very Mozarts on our favourite instruments. But my bell-ringing practice was shortened by a singular accident, which not only stopped my performance, but made even the sound of a bell terrible to my ears.

One Sunday I went with another into the belfry to ring for noon prayers, but the second stroke we had pulled showed us that the clapper of the bell we were at was muffled. Someone had been buried that morning, and it had been prepared, of course, to ring a mournful note. We did not know of this, but the remedy was easy.

"Jack," said my companion, "step up to the loft and cut off the hat"; for the way we had of muffling was by tying a piece of an old hat, or of cloth (the former was preferred), to one side of the clapper, which deadened every second toll.

"*I succeeded in jumping down, and throwing myself on the flat of my back under the bell.*"

I complied, and, mounting into the belfry, crept as usual into the bell, where I began to cut away. The hat had been tied on in some more complicated manner than usual, and I was perhaps three or four minutes in getting it off, during which time my companion below was hastily called away, by a message from his sweetheart, I believe; but that is not material to my story.

The person who called him was a brother of the club, who, knowing that the time had come for ringing for service, and not thinking that anyone was above, began to pull. At this moment I was just getting out, when I felt the bell moving. I guessed the reason at once—it was a moment of terror; but by a hasty, and almost convulsive effort, I succeeded in jumping down, and throwing myself on the flat of my back under the bell.

The room in which it was was little more than sufficient to contain it, the bottom of the bell coming within a couple of feet of the floor of lath. At that time I certainly was not so bulky as I am now, but as I lay it was within an inch of my face. I had not laid myself down a second when the ringing began. It was a dreadful situation. Over me swung an immense mass of metal, one touch of which would have crushed me to pieces; the floor under me was principally composed of crazy laths, and if they gave way, I was precipitated to the distance of about fifty feet upon a loft, which would, in all probability, have sunk under the impulse of my fall, and sent me to be dashed to atoms upon the marble floor of the chancel, a hundred feet below.

I remembered—for fear is quick in recollection—how a common clockwright, about a month before, had fallen, and, bursting through the floors of the steeple, driven in the ceilings of the porch, and even broken into the marble tombstone of a bishop who slept beneath. This was my first terror, but the ringing had not continued a minute before a more awful and immediate dread came on me. The deafening sound of the bell smote into my ears with a thunder which made me fear their drums would crack. There was not a fibre of my body it did not thrill through; it entered my very soul; thought and reflection were almost banished; I only retained the sensation of agonising terror.

Every moment I saw the bell sweep within an inch of my face; and my eyes—I could not close them, though to look at the object was bitter as death—followed it instinctively in its oscillating progress until it came back again. It was in vain I said to myself that it could come no nearer at any future swing than it did at first; every time it descended I endeavoured to shrink into the very floor to avoid being buried under the down-sweeping mass; and then reflecting on the danger of pressing too weightily on my frail support, would cower up again as far as I dared.

At first my fears were mere matter of fact. I was afraid the pulleys above would give way and let the bell plunge on me. At another time the possibility of the clapper being shot out in some sweep, and dashing through my body, as I had seen a ramrod glide through a door, flitted across my mind. The dread also, as I have already mentioned, of the crazy floor, tormented me; but these soon gave way to fears not more unfounded, but more visionary, and of course more tremendous. The roaring of the bell confused my intellect, and my fancy soon began to teem with all sorts of strange and terrifying ideas. The bell pealing above, and opening its jaws with a hideous clamour, seemed to me at one time a ravening monster, raging to devour me; at another, a whirlpool ready to suck me into its bellowing abyss.

As I gazed on it, it assumed all shapes; it was a flying eagle, or rather a roc of the Arabian story-tellers, clapping its wings and screaming over me. As I looked upwards into it, it would appear sometimes to lengthen into indefinite extent, or to be twisted at the end into the spiral folds of the tail of a flying-dragon. Nor was the flaming breath, or fiery glance of that fabled animal, wanting to complete the picture. My eyes, inflamed, bloodshot, and glaring, invested the supposed monster with a full proportion of unholy light.

It would be endless were I to merely hint at all the fancies that possessed my mind. Every object that was hideous and roaring presented itself to my imagination. I often thought that I was in a hurricane at sea, and that the vessel in which I was embarked tossed under me with the most furious vehemence. The air, set in

"*At last the devil himself made his appearance.*"

motion by the swinging of the bell, blew over me, nearly with the violence, and more than the thunder of a tempest; and the floor seemed to reel under me, as under a drunken man.

But the most awful of all the ideas that seized on me were drawn from the supernatural. In the vast cavern of the bell hideous faces appeared, and glared down on me with terrifying frowns, or with grinning mockery, still more appalling. At last the devil himself, accoutred, as in the common description of the evil spirit, with hoof, horn and tail, and eyes of infernal lustre, made his appearance, and called on me to curse God and worship him, who was powerful to save me. This dread suggestion he uttered with the full-toned clangour of the bell. I had him within an inch of me and I thought on the fate of the Santon Barsisa. Strenuously and desperately I defied him, and bade him be gone.

Reason then, for a moment, resumed her sway, but it was only to fill me with fresh terror, just as the lightning dispels the gloom that surrounds the benighted mariner, but to show him that his vessel is driving on a rock, where she must inevitably be dashed to pieces. I found I was becoming delirious, and trembled lest reason should utterly desert me. This is at all times an agonising thought, but it smote me then with tenfold agony. I feared lest, when utterly deprived of my senses, I should rise, to do which I was every moment tempted by that strange feeling which calls on a man, whose head is dizzy from standing on the battlement of a lofty castle, to precipitate himself from it, and then death would be instant and tremendous.

When I thought of this I became desperate. I caught the floor with a grasp which drove the blood from my nails; and I yelled with the cry of despair. I called for help, I prayed, I shouted, but all the efforts of my voice were, of course, drowned in the bell. As it passed over my mouth it occasionally echoed my cries, which mixed not with its own sound, but preserved their distinct character. Perhaps this was but fancy. To me, I know, they then sounded as if they were the shouting, howling, or laughing of the fiends with which my imagination had peopled the gloomy cave which swung over me.

12

You may accuse me of exaggerating my feelings; but I am not. Many a scene of dread have I since passed through, but they are nothing to the self-inflicted terrors of this half-hour. The ancients have doomed one of the damned in their Tartarus to lie under a rock, which every moment seems to be descending to annihilate him—and an awful punishment it would be. But if to this you add a clamour as loud as if ten thousand furies were howling about you—a deafening uproar banishing reason, and driving you to madness, you must allow that the bitterness of the pang was rendered more terrible. There is no man, firm as his nerves may be, who could retain his courage in this situation.

In twenty minutes the ringing was done. Half of that time passed over me without power of computation—the other half appeared an age. When it ceased, I became gradually more quiet, but a new fear retained me. I knew that five minutes would elapse without ringing, but at the end of that short time the bell would be rung a second time, for five minutes more. I could not calculate time. A minute and an hour were of equal duration. I feared to rise, lest the five minutes should have elapsed, and the ringing be again commenced, in which case I should be crushed, before I could escape, against the walls or framework of the bell. I therefore still continued to lie down, cautiously shifting myself, however, with a careful gliding, so that my eye no longer looked into the hollow.

This was of itself a considerable relief. The cessation of the noise had, in a great measure, the effect of stupefying me, for my attention, being no longer occupied by the chimeras I had conjured up, began to flag. All that now distressed me was the constant expectation of the second ringing, for which, however, I settled myself with a kind of stupid resolution. I closed my eyes, and clenched my teeth as firmly as if they were screwed in a vice. At last the dreaded moment came, and the first swing of the bell extorted a groan from me, as they say the most resolute victim screams at the sight of the rack, to which he is for a second time destined. After this, however, I lay silent and lethargic, without a thought. Wrapped in the defensive armour of stupidity, I defied

13

the bell and its intonations. When it ceased, I was roused a little by the hope of escape. I did not, however, decide on this step hastily, but, putting up my hand with the utmost caution, I touched the rim.

Though the ringing had ceased, it still was tremulous from the sound, and shook under my hand, which instantly recoiled as from an electric jar. A quarter of an hour probably elapsed before I again dared to make the experiment, and then I found it at rest. I determined to lose no time, fearing that I might have delayed already too long, and that the bell for evening service would catch me. This dread stimulated me, and I slipped out with the utmost rapidity and arose. I stood, I suppose, for a minute, looking with silly wonder on the place of my imprisonment, penetrated with the joy of escaping, but then rushed down the stony and irregular stair with the velocity of lightning and arrived in the bellringer's room. This was the last act I had power to accomplish. I leaned against the wall, motionless and deprived of thought, in which posture my companions found me, when in the course of a couple of hours, they returned to their occupation. They were shocked, as well they might, at the figure before them. The wind of the bell had excoriated my face, and my dim and stupefied eyes were fixed with a lack-lustre gaze in my raw eyelids. My hands were torn and bleeding, my hair dishevelled, and my clothes tattered. They spoke to me, but I gave no answer. They shook me, but I remained insensible. They then became alarmed, and hastened to remove me. He who had first gone up with me in the forenoon met them as they carried me through the churchyard, and through him, who was shocked at having, in some measure, occasioned the accident, the cause of my misfortune was discovered. I was put to bed at home, and remained for three days delirious, but gradually recovered my senses.

You may be sure the bell formed a prominent topic of my ravings, and if I heard a peal, they were instantly increased to the utmost violence. Even when the delirium abated, my sleep was continually disturbed by imagined ringings, and my dreams were haunted by the fancies which almost maddened me while in the steeple. My friends removed me to a house in the country, which was sufficiently distant from any place of worship to save me from the apprehensions of hearing the church-going bell; for what Alexander Selkirk, in Cowper's poem, complained of as a misfortune, was then to me as a blessing.

Here I recovered; but, even long after recovery, if a gale wafted the notes of a peal towards me, I started with nervous apprehension. I felt a Mahometan hatred to all the bell tribe, and envied the subjects of the Commander of the Faithful the sonorous voice of their Muezzin. Time cured this, as it does the most of our follies; but, even at the present day, if, by chance, my nerves be unstrung, some particular tones of the cathedral bell have power to surprise me into a momentary start.

Trapped in a Floating Tomb

by ROBERT DE LA CROIX

At the end of the month of April, 1903, the crews of vessels calling at ports along the Prussian coast reported a strange object encountered at sea. They had several times noticed it, sometimes glittering in the sunshine, sometimes gleaming dully when the sky was overcast. It looked something like a buoy, a sort of metallic bell, or else the capsized hull of a ship.

They could not quite make out what it was. And, unfortunately, none of those who had encountered it could get near enough to identify the thing, either on account of bad weather, which made them fear a collision, or because they had no time to investigate it.

The maritime authorities at Memel and Danzig had been warned of the presence of this mysterious flotsam, but they seemed in no hurry to take the matter up. It was not so much that they disbelieved the tale as that they could not be bothered, or did not possess the equipment necessary to proceed with an inquiry. After all, there would be no end to it if one started getting excited about all the wreckage floating about at sea, especially near the coast.

On Thursday, April 30th, towards the end of the afternoon, the Norwegian sailing-ship *Aurora* also sighted this enigmatic object, some sixteen miles off Dixhoeft. The sea was calm, and, as

16

"It looked something like a buoy, a sort of metallic bell, or else the capsized hull of a ship."

there seemed no risk in approaching closer, Captain Soerensen bore down.

At ten yards' range, he came to the conclusion that it was undoubtedly the metal hull of a capsized vessel, probably a small schooner. He wondered what dramatic events had preceded the wreck.

To be capsized or dismasted is the most terrible fate that can befall a sailing ship. The crew, then, has little or no chance of survival. Soerensen could imagine the steersman convulsively gripping the wheel, the seamen hurled violently overboard. As for those who happened to be below at the time, it was to be hoped that they had been quick enough, instinctively, to dash on deck through the hatchway and spring overboard. Otherwise, well . . .

The blank, sinister appearance of that capsized hull gave the crew of the *Aurora* a queer feeling. It even frightened them, though they had really no reason to fear it.

"Well, we can't stay here all night," one of them said. "It was a bad business, that's certain. But we can't do anything about it now."

"Shut up!" bawled Soerensen.

There was no need to ask why he had called for silence. In the twilight stillness, the men fancied they could hear something like faint but distinct blows struck on the plating of the hull. At first they could only catch the sound of one at a time. Then the rapping came faster, as though some impatient caller were knocking with his fist on a closed door.

"It's only the water lapping round the old hulk," one of the sailors observed.

But mere ripples could hardly make such a noise as that. It started again, louder still, sounding like dull, metallic drum-taps.

"I don't see how you can say that's water," someone objected. "Each one of those taps is distinct and separate, like the blows of a hammer."

"Well, then; it's something rattling about inside the thing."

"Maybe," retorted Soerensen. "But I'm going to find out. Lower the boat and bring a gaff along. We'll soon see what it is."

18

The *Aurora's* boat moved slowly round the wreck. The mysterious sounds had ceased. Soerensen seized the boat-hook and struck the hull of the derelict several times with it. The boat drew off a little under the impacts.

"We'd better make fast to the thing. Find something to hitch her on to, one of you," Soerensen ordered.

Easier said than done. The hull of the wreck presented a smooth, unrelieved surface.

"All right then," said the skipper. "Try to climb aboard. I'll pass you the gaff."

The man addressed, after taking off his boots and stockings, finally managed to stand upright on the hull. He struck a number of smart blows on it with the boat-hook, stopped, and then started again.

"That's right. Stop. Now listen."

The mysterious sounds became audible once more, like a muffled echo, but on a deeper note. As before, they consisted of faint, but distinctly separate, taps.

"Begin again!" cried Soerensen.

The boat-hook resumed its rattling against the hull, then ceased. At once the strange echoes replied. But this time they sounded more agitated.

"There's someone inside!" exclaimed Soerensen. "He's signalling to us! He's calling for help!"

"But hang it all, skipper," the seaman retorted, "ships have been reporting the wreck for a week on end. Anyone inside must have died long ago."

The rest of the crew made no comment. They felt sceptical and yet decidedly uneasy. It seemed impossible that any human being could have survived imprisonment in that hulk, with no air to breathe or food to eat.

All the same, that obstinate, desperate rapping was still going on. It was followed by what seemed a faint shout, deadened by the intervening metal.

"We're all dreaming. It can't be true," one of the *Aurora's* crew said.

19

Soerensen did not answer. He circled the wreck again in his boat. No; it would not be possible, with the equipment he had available, to make any sort of an opening in the hull. And yet he could not leave those poor wretches, if there really were any there, to die in that floating tomb.

The sea was still calm and the coast was near. Why not try to tow the wreck into Danzig? The port authorities there would be able to cut the hull open and find out the source of those mysterious sounds.

Soerensen succeeded in making a tow-line fast astern. As night fell, the *Aurora* set a course for Danzig, trailing the wreck behind her. No sound came from the derelict now.

At dawn on May 1st, the *Aurora*, with the capsized schooner in tow, was moored in the outer harbour at Danzig. The passage had been a slow and anxious one. Soerensen had never ceased to fear that the hull might sink, but the baulks of timber, which had formed part of her cargo, kept the hull afloat, acting as a kind of lifebelt.

All night long, those aboard the *Aurora* had listened in silence for a repetition of those strange rappings from the wreck's interior. But nothing more had been heard. Were the prisoners asleep? Had they understood that they were being rescued and that it was therefore useless to go on signalling? Or had that tapping only been the last of their efforts before they died? Perhaps they were now lying prostrate, in a state of exhaustion, devoting their last thoughts to those rescuers who had arrived too late, by a few hours only, to save their lives.

The derelict now lay alongside the quay, but the captain of the port, fearing that she might sink, had steel cables slung under her and made an attempt to raise the hull with a crane. He brought it about a yard higher out of the water and resecured it in that position, where he judged it would be safe enough.

Then he had a blow-pipe applied to the plates. The men worked in a shower of sparks, to the accompaniment of the roar of the flames attacking the metal. They reminded one of the

20

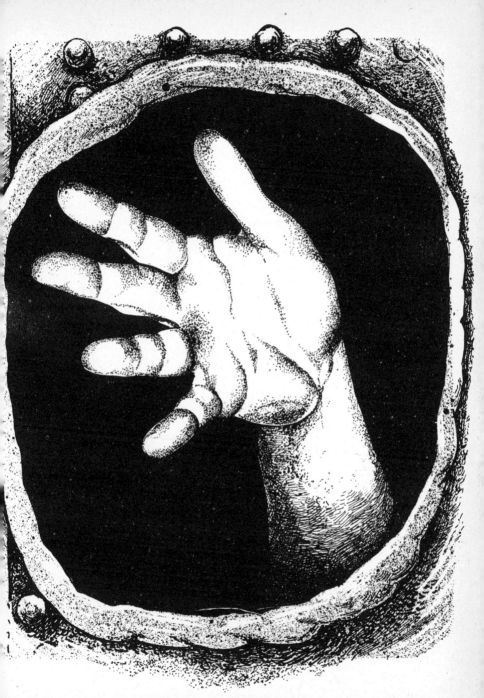

"It was a man's hand."

alchemists of yore crouching over a retort; one which, in this case, had a mystery of the sea to reveal.

As the work approached completion, the crowd of onlookers on the quays increased. They gazed inquisitively and apprehensively at the strange hull. Now that the stern was above water, they could read its name—the *Erndte*, of Hamburg. She had been a coastal schooner frequenting the Baltic and the North Sea and was well known in the harbour at Danzig.

After an hour's work, a small rectangle had been cut away from the plating. All those engaged in the operation stared eagerly at the shadowy opening through which they expected the wreck's secret to emerge.

One minute passed.

No one moved. It was as though they all feared to look into that gaping hole, still more to call through it, in case some astonishing or terrifying picture should meet their gaze or their cries evoke nothing but tragic silence. If anyone were still alive down there, surely he would start up when he saw daylight and shout for help.

Yet nothing was to be seen and nothing was to be heard. The next step must be of course, to enter the hull and investigate. But the workmen, in their haste, had made only a small opening, too narrow to admit a man's body.

The captain of the port, after consulting Soerensen, signed to the workmen. They took up the blow-pipes again. Suddenly a murmur went up from the crowd. It rose to a shout. The spectators were gesticulating. One of them was even clapping his hands as though applauding a well—mounted scene on the stage.

Something white had appeared at the opening in the hull. It remained motionless for a few seconds, then began to move slowly along one of the sides of the rectangular space. It trembled, grew bigger.

It was a man's hand. The spread fingers became clearly visible, then a gesticulating sleeve. It seemed to be waving a greeting to the sunlight, to life, to the watching crowd. It was as

22

though the arm of one raised from the dead were emerging from a tomb.

The spectators, rigid with amazement, remained motionless, staring as if turned to stone. They could not believe that anyone could have survived inside such a floating wreck for more than a week. The thing was surely impossible. It must be a case of collective hallucination.

The Talking Hand

Suddenly someone called out: "The hand's talking!"

No one dreamed of laughing. For it was true enough. A deep, breathless, harshly distorted voice was coming from the depths of that ruin of a ship, demanding something, and with anguish. "I want to eat. Give me something to eat!"

The spell was broken. Several people rushed forward, carrying loaves of bread or bottles of beer. It was true! There was someone there, someone with a desperate will to live, who had survived, by a miracle, that deadly struggle with hunger, thirst and airlessness. The hand seized the victuals offered and disappeared.

"Enlarge that opening, quick!" Soerensen ordered.

Work was resumed, this time with eager zest. It was now certain that at least one survivor remained aboard. An astonishing case! Crews had, of course, often enough been found alive aboard a wreck, but they had been able to breathe freely, eat, and hope to meet other vessels. And they could make signals of distress. The fact that a man had managed to survive inside that sealed hull was a unique, incredible and almost supernatural circumstance.

The crowd watched the work of enlargement with feverish impatience. But it took time—a very considerable time. Two hours went by, then three. When the men stopped to rest for a few moments, more food was passed through the aperture, and encouraging messages were shouted down. At last, about eleven o'clock, an area of about a square yard had been cut away. A volunteer dropped through it. He saw a man, one man only, about thirty-five years old, lying on sailcloth in a corner of the hold. His face was covered with brown hair. An empty cask and a wooden mallet, battered and flattened with incessant use, lay at his feet. A rope with twelve knots in it could be seen behind him.

Tale of Terror

"Been here for twelve days," he mumbled. "Name's Hans Engellandt, master of the schooner *Erndte*. My crew were on deck when the vessel capsized. Were you able to rescue any of them?"

The *Erndte*, a steel-built schooner of eighty tons, had left Memel two weeks before. She was bound for Bremen with a cargo of deal planks. Hans Engellandt was both commander and owner of the vessel, which had a crew of four.

They had bad luck from the start. A violent squall from the northwest struck the schooner abeam and flooded the cargo. Engellandt had great difficulty in keeping on his course.

At seven o'clock that evening, the sea, which had been running high all day, lashed itself into a frenzy. The *Erndte* rolled madly, occasionally even disappearing for a few seconds, then painfully righting herself.

Engellandt shortened sail. The vessel could then be better controlled. She made good time all that night, but suffered heavy damage. At five o'clock in the morning, the log showed that she had covered one hundred and twenty miles since leaving Memel. The first glimmers of daybreak revealed a sea white with foam all round the ship. Engellandt was gripping the wheel. He was soaked through, stiff and bruised, shivering with cold and fatigue. Feeling faint, he ordered the mate, though the sea was still running high, to steer the vessel for a few moments while he changed his clothes and swallowed a little food. Before going down the hatch, he took a last look round. Clouds were piling up to the east, in the dim light of the approaching day, and it seemed to be blowing harder than ever.

24

The mate stood at the wheel, motionless. One of the crew was keeping a look-out at the cathead, protected by an awning from the flying spray. The cargo seemed to be holding firm against the repeated assaults of the waves.

Well, thought the captain, it would be a stiff passage, but they ought to get through to Bremen all right. On reaching his cabin, he was at last able to put on dry clothing.

He fancied, in that confined space, that the ship's movements were growing more violent. At first he thought he might be mistaken. Then, as he listened more intently to the waves thundering against the vessel's side and the wind whistling through her rigging, he knew he was right. The storm was rising to a hurricane.

He was leaning forward to pull on his boots when his head, as though punched by an invisible fist, banged against the cabin bulkhead. At the same time, the whole of the schooner quivered under a violent shock, and a fantastic uproar, composed of the clatter of falling objects broken to pieces, the crash of torrential waves and the shouts of his men, deafened him from above.

He believed the sounds were due to injury to his hearing, sustained as a result of the terrific blow struck against his head. He struggled to his feet and began to look for his storm-lantern, which had gone out. He tripped over the four legs of an overturned chair and a lot of smashed crockery.

The howling of the tempest now took on a deeper note, as though Engellandt had been cut off from the outside world by a partition of some kind. Even the recurrent thunders of the squalls reached his ears in a deadened echo, as though he were wrapped in cotton-wool. He could not hear the whistling of the shrouds at all. "Must have been dismasted," he muttered, with a shudder.

He groped for the hatch-ladder in order to climb on deck. But he couldn't find it. He passed the palm of his hand carefully over the four walls of his cabin, staggering about among the chairs and other objects that had fallen to the floor. Apparently the ladder had vanished.

25

I suppose it dropped when she rolled just now, thought Engellandt. Well, never mind; I can pull myself up to the hatch somehow.

Climbing on to a chair, he tried to find the hatch. He had closed it when he came down, to prevent the cabin being flooded. He felt all over the ceiling with his hands, just as he had previously felt the walls. The hatch ought to be in the corner for'ard, to port.

But Engellandt had now lost his bearings altogether. He tried to identify each corner, one after the other. In the first he found nothing. Nor in the second. Must be in the third, then. No; it wasn't. Well then, in the fourth—no. There, too, the deckhead was perfectly smooth, without the least trace of a hatchway.

Engellandt felt that he must be dreaming. For an instant he believed, absurdly enough, that he was dead. He could only hear relatively faint sounds now. Finally, he pulled himself together. Whatever the answer to this mystery might be, he was alive and uninjured.

He made up his mind that he would really have to use his eyes. He found his lamp, then discovered that its base was wet. Water must have penetrated the cabin when the ship had rolled so heavily.

He struck a match and put it to the wick. In the ensuing smoky glare he could see nothing at first but the walls of the cabin, tremulous in the uncertain light. Then he raised the lamp to examine the ceiling, still with the idea of finding the hatch. His rigid arm wavered as he tried with all his strength to master the onset of panic. This time there was no doubt about it. The hatch had vanished!

He continued to move the lamp to and fro mechanically, but without hope. The hatch was definitely not there.

His legs were shaking. He groped at the wall for support, then, with the intention of sitting down, grasped a fallen chair and tried to set it upright.

It wouldn't stand properly. Something on the floor was in its way. He made an attempt to kick the obstacle aside. But it seemed to be a kind of frame fixed to the floor itself.

26

He shone the lamp down at it, then gave a violent start. It was the hatch! He was standing on the hatch which ought to have been above his head!

He realised that he had been walking on the deckhead, not the floor. That could only mean that the ship had capsized!

The roll that had thrown him against the bulkhead had turned the *Erndte* upside down. The keel was above him now, like a roof, with an implacable pressure he would never be able to remove. The cargo of timber kept the vessel afloat. But she was now a prison in which, in all probability, he was doomed to remain until he died.

Suddenly he remembered his crew. They would be swimming now, no doubt, with desperate anxiety round and round the walls of his prison, battling with the icy water. He thought of calling out to them. But the idea only made him shrug his shoulders. What was the use? Even if they heard him, what could they do for him? In any case, they had probably been drowned by this time.

Fight with Fate

He shrugged with cold or with terror. It might have been either. Nevertheless, despite his anguish, he never dreamed for a single instant of resigning himself to his fate. On the contrary, all he feared was an increase in the violence of the storm, though any such event would soon have cut short the inevitable torments of the lingering death to which he seemed to be doomed.

By the light of his lamp he marked the waterline on one of the uprights in the wall. Then he dislodged, with an iron lever, a number of the floorboards overhead. He meant to make his way into the hold, see what he could find there to help him to survive, and do what he could, with the means available in that part of the ship, to keep her afloat.

The *Erndte* carried no cargo except timber. The ballast consisted of a mass of lead casting firmly riveted in position and unlikely to come adrift.

Looking down into the cabin, Engellandt saw that water was entering it to port or starboard, according to the direction in which the ship rolled. Boxes and splinters of wood were floating about. Obviously the cabin would soon be uninhabitable. He decided to stay in the hold, where he would at least be dry.

The *Erndte* measured eleven feet, vertically, below deck. The cabin was seven feet high. Consequently, Engellandt calculated that he was only four feet from the keel. He could only sit or lie. But at any rate he would be relatively safe if he stayed where he was.

He lay down for a few moments. He could hear the waves raging round the ship, buffeting her until she rolled, and breaking over her. How long would his imprisonment last? What were the chances of his coming out alive? It must be already light outside by this time. Some vessels would be sure to sight the capsized hull and approach it to investigate. Then he would find means to make his presence known.

But when would that be? How many days could he stand living like this?

Echo of Despair

He realised that as he would not be able to see ships in the neighbourhood he would have to try to attract attention without waiting any longer. He shouted. The metal walls of the hold flung his voice back at him He seized a heavy piece of wood and struck the wall with it. He felt sure that the sound would be more clearly audible outside than any shout. The clang it made would be like a gong resounding over the waters. It would be certain to arouse the interests of a possible rescuer.

He went down into the cabin again so as to be able to stand upright, and began banging on its walls with the wooden mallet, again and again, as hard as he could, with mounting vexation and, at last, despair. Planting his legs far apart to balance himself against the rolling of the ship, he continued this exercise until he was exhausted.

The storm raged on and on. He realised that the roar of the wind would certainly drown his hammering on the hull. Consequently, vessels that sighted the wreck would not hear his blows, and would undoubtedly make off so as to avoid a collision, rather than approach.

He ceased his efforts, concluding that he would have to remain a prisoner until the weather improved.

He returned to the hold, noticing that the sea-level had not risen. The fact comforted him. He searched the victualling store. A box of biscuits had fallen into the water on the cabin floor, or rather, deckhead. The beer bottles were all broken. After a long search, he managed to salvage three pounds of raisins, some sugar and sausage-meat, a flask of brandy and a keg of drinking-water.

He stowed these provisions carefully away in the hold, making sure they would not come adrift. They represented his sole chance of survival.

He then took stock of the situation again. At least he need not fear death by starvation—not for the moment, at any rate. Moreover, the capsized hull was unlikely to sink. So far, so good. But what about air to breathe? Would he not be likely to suffocate, after absorbing all the oxygen available?

He decided, accordingly, to put out the lamp, so as not to waste air. But in the darkness his terror and mental torments returned. Nevertheless he gradually got used to the obscurity, relieved as it was to a certain extent by the glimmers of the water in the cabin.

The changes in their intensity enabled him to measure the passage of time. When the water turned black, he guessed that night had fallen, made a knot in a rope, wrapped himself in sailcloth in a corner of the hold and tried to sleep.

Sometimes he woke up suddenly, believing that he heard a ship approaching. He would then begin again to thump the walls with his mallet, with wild violence, until exhaustion set in. Then, supposing he had been mistaken, he would lie down again, a prey to a succession of nightmares and to the tortures of hunger and thirst.

29

"He resumed his efforts with the mallet."

He instinctively tried to conjecture what course the wreck might be taking. Judging by the currents prevalent in that area, he believed he must be drifting south-south-east.

At last the storm began to die down. Acordingly he resumed his efforts with the mallet. But the meagre diet had undermined his strength, and he had to abandon them more and more often, in a state of exhaustion, to lie down once more, with a painfully beating heart.

The rope now had six knots in it. He had been a prisoner in the wreck for six days.

The weather had turned fine once more, and the sky must have been cloudless, with the sun blazing down on the hull, for the atmosphere in the hold was growing hotter. Soon it became a suffocating torment, crushing him with a fearful weight of depression. He went down to the cabin to try to obtain some relief from the coolness of the water. He bent over its surface, fascinated by its slow, rhythmic movements, corresponding with the rolling of the wreck. He bent lower and lower.

The water offered him not only relief from the clammy heat beating down from the steel plates of the hull, but also oblivion, in which he could forget his terrible nightmare of a prison, from which there was no way out.

As he leaned closer to the water, he longed to let himself drop into its cool depths, with their promise of forgetfulness and the cessation of all toil and anguish. He leaned lower and lower.

Then he noticed that the slow, oscillating movements of the liquid had changed to faster ones. That could only mean that the wind was rising again.

The new, rapid rhythm revived his enervated faculties, breaking the spell that had been lulling his brain. It occurred to him that the rising wind would reduce temperature and put an end to his sufferings from the heat.

He was right. Soon he was able to climb back into the hold. That evening he tied another knot in the rope. It was the eleventh.

31

His keg of fresh water was almost empty. There was nothing left of his provisions but a little sugar, a handful of rice and a slice or two of sausage.

How much longer could he hold out? Two days at most, perhaps. He continued to rap on the walls, but by this time his mallet was so worn as to be almost useless.

"I must keep going, keep going," he told himself repeatedly, aloud. But he could not see how he was to do so, or why, indeed, he should not despair.

The wreck must be drifting in frequented waters. It must certainly have been sighted. But no one seemed to have had the idea of salvaging it. Engellandt understood the reason. Derelicts were shunned. Their sinister outlines were avoided like the plague. Who could dream that this one contained a captive desperately struggling, against all logic and probability, to survive, to conquer a fate that seemed inevitable?

He was utterly prostrated now, only just able to breathe in the contaminated air. The end could not be far off, he was certain.

Then with a shock, he suddenly saw clearly that he would never be rescued by others. His only chance would be to escape from this appalling prison by taking an extremely risky step, but one which might succeed and which he had been thinking of for a long time. He might try to force back the door of the cabin, dive into the sea and swim up to the surface.

He had hesitated until then to adopt this desperate expedient, for even if he succeeded in it, he would be too weak to swim for long, even if he supported himself on the wreck. But all he would have to fear would be a quicker and less painful death than that which awaited him if he did not take the risk. He decided, therefore, to take it.

He dived into the swirling water in the cabin, found the door, after blindly groping for it, and tried to shift it. Then he felt himself suffocating, and regained the surface to breathe. Again he dived, thrusting at the door with his shoulder. But the weight of water behind it was too much for him.

Engellandt felt that all the sinister powers of the ocean were in

32

league against him, preventing his escape. In the end, in fact, despite repeated efforts, he was obliged to return to the hold once more. He lay there with a confused buzzing in his ears, utterly crushed, this time, by the sheer malignity of his fate. The rope hung beside him. By its reckoning, the day was April 30th.

He gazed dully at the darkening surface, indicating the approach of night, of the water in the cabin. The sea must have been quite calm, for the wreck of the *Erndte*, possibly for the first time since the original storm, had ceased to roll. Complete silence enveloped her.

In that utter stillness, he lost his will to resist. He was no longer even tempted to seize the stump of his mallet and thump frantically with it, shriek and sob, as he had so often when, with his ear pressed to the wall, he had fancied he could hear the sound of a wake or of a propeller thrashing the waves.

He began to lose consciousness, dreaming of the open sea, dotted with white sails, under a summer sun. A ship was bearing down on him. He was hailed: "Who are you?"... "I am Hans Engellandt," he replied. "Master of the *Erndte*. I was making for Bremen with a cargo of timber. We sank. I have been dead for nearly a fortnight. I was thirty-five when I died, betrayed by my own ship. I am the prisoner of a wreck. Keep off, or she'll sink you."

He had become delirious. He was experiencing the extraordinary sensation of being surrounded by the echo of his own blood, the beating of his own heart, reverberating in every quarter of the hull.

Suddenly, the strange sounds ceased. "I am dead," Engellandt murmured. "My heart must have left my body already. And now it has stopped beating altogether."

Then the sounds started again. Engellandt, with a convulsive shudder, regained consciousness. What was this? Yes, those were blows—blows delivered against the hull—from outside!

He remained motionless for a few moments, not daring to believe his ears. When the sound ceased again he fancied he really had been suffering from hallucination. But when they started

33

once more, accompanied by exclamations in human speech, he seized his mallet and struck in his turn, at first in a confused sort of manner, mingling the blows of the mallet with plaintive cries and hammering on the wall with his fist.

Then he realised that he ought to proceed more methodically, that he ought to reply firmly and distinctly to the blows he heard, and try to make himself understood. He could still hear voices. But the words were unintelligible to him. His head was in a whirl.

Panic seized him. He was quite certain this time that there were men near the wreck. And yet, perhaps, they were about to go away, thinking they had been mistaken in supposing they had heard sounds from it. Or else they merely meant to report what they had found, and the wreck would eventually be towed into harbour.

But when? More and more days of this?

"I can't hold out any longer!" he shouted. "Come to my assistance instantly!"

He waited for an answer. None came.

In a state of collapse, he lay down again on the sailcloth. After a few minutes' rest, he went down to the cabin and again wrestled with the door. It still resisted all his efforts. He climbed back into the hold, half drowned, and lost consciousness once more.

He was still asleep when the *Aurora*, with the wreck in tow, entered Neufahrwasser, the outer harbour of the port of Danzig. He did not hear the murmurs of the crowd and the preparations for his rescue. But when the first blow-pipes were applied to the hull of the *Erndte* he opened his eyes, thinking that sunlight had begun to filter into the wreck, preparatory to flooding it with those rays from which he had been so long absent.

An Occurrence at Owl Creek Bridge

by AMBROSE BIERCE

A man stood upon a railroad bridge in northern Alabama, looking down into the swift water twenty feet below. The man's hands were behind his back, the wrists bound with a cord. A rope closely encircled his neck. It was attached to a stout cross-timber above his head and the slack fell to the level of his knees. Some loose boards laid upon the sleepers supporting the metals of the railway supplied a footing for him and his executioners—two private soldiers of the Federal army, directed by a sergeant who in civil life may have been a deputy sheriff. At a short remove upon the same temporary platform was an officer in the uniform of his rank, armed. He was a captain. A sentinel at each end of the bridge stood with his rifle in the position known as "support", that is to say, vertical in front of the left shoulder, the hammer resting on the forearm thrown straight across the chest—a formal and unnatural position, enforcing an erect carriage of the body. It did not appear to be the duty of these two men to know what was occurring at the centre of the bridge; they merely blockaded the two ends of the foot planking that traversed it.

Beyond one of the sentinels nobody was in sight; the railroad ran straight away into a forest for a hundred yards, then, curving, was lost to view. Doubtless there was an outpost farther

"The man's hands were behind his back. A rope closely encircled his neck."

along. The other bank of the stream was open ground—a gentle acclivity topped with a stockade of vertical tree trunks, loopholed for rifles, with a single embrasure through which protruded the muzzle of a brass cannon commanding the bridge. Midway of the slope between bridge and fort were the spectators—a single company of infantry in line, at "parade rest", the butts of the rifles on the ground, the barrels inclining slightly backwards against the right shoulder, the hands crossed upon the stock. A lieutenant stood at the right of the line, the point of his sword upon the ground, his left hand resting upon his right. Excepting the group of four at the centre of the bridge, not a man moved. The company faced the ridge, staring stonily, motionless. The sentinels, facing the banks of the stream, might have been statues to adorn the bridge. The captain stood with folded arms, silent, observing the work of his subordinates, but making no sign. Death is a dignitary who when he comes announced is to be received with formal manifestations of respect, even by those most familiar with him. In the code of military etiquette silence and fixity are forms of deference.

The man who was engaged in being hanged was apparently about thirty-five years of age. He was a civilian, if one might judge from his habit, which was that of a planter. His features were good—a straight nose, firm mouth, broad forehead, from which his long dark hair was combed straight back, falling behind his ears to the collar of his well-fitting frock-coat. He wore a moustache and pointed beard, but no whiskers; his eyes were large and dark grey, and had a kindly expression which one would hardly have expected in one whose neck was in the hemp. Evidently this was no vulgar assassin. The liberal military code makes provision for hanging many kinds of persons, and gentlemen are not excluded.

The preparations being complete, the two private soldiers stepped aside and each drew away the plank upon which he had been standing. The sergeant turned to the captain, saluted and placed himself immediately behind that officer, who in turn moved apart one pace. These movements left the condemned

37

man and the sergeant standing on the two ends of the same plank, which spanned three of the cross-ties of the bridge. The end upon which the civilian stood almost, but not quite, reached a fourth. This plank had been held in place by the weight of the captain; it was now held by that of the sergeant. At a signal from the former the latter would step aside, the plank would tilt and the condemned man go down between two ties. The arrangement commended itself to his judgement as simple and effective. His face had not been covered nor his eyes bandaged. He looked a moment at his "unsteadfast footing", then let his gaze wander to the swirling water of the stream racing madly beneath his feet. A piece of dancing driftwood caught his attention and his eyes followed it down the current. How slowly it appeared to move! What a sluggish stream!

He closed his eyes in order to fix his last thoughts upon his wife and children. The water, touched to gold by the early sun, the brooding mists under the banks at some distance down the stream, the fort, the soldiers, the piece of drift—all had distracted him. And now he became conscious of a new disturbance. Striking through the thought of his dear ones was a sound which he could neither ignore nor understand, a sharp, distinct, metallic percussion like the stroke of a blacksmith's hammer upon the anvil; it had the same ringing quality. He wondered what it was, and whether immeasurably distant or nearby—it seemed both. Its recurrence was regular, but as slow as the tolling of a death knell. He awaited each stroke with impatience and—he knew not why—apprehension. The intervals of silence grew progressively longer; the delays became maddening. With their greater infrequency the sounds increased in strength and sharpness. They hurt his ear like the thrust of a knife; he feared he would shriek. What he heard was the ticking of his watch.

He unclosed his eyes and saw again the water below him. "If I could free my hands," he thought, "I might throw off the noose and spring into the stream. By diving I could evade the bullets and, swimming vigorously, reach the bank, take to the woods and get away home. My home, thank God, is as yet outside their lines;

my wife and little ones are still beyond the invader's farthest advance."

As these thoughts, which have here to be set down in words, were flashed into the doomed man's brain rather than evolved from it the captain nodded to the sergeant. The sergeant stepped aside.

Peyton Farquhar was a well-to-do planter, of an old and highly respected Alabama family. Being a slave owner and like other slave owners a politician, he was naturally an original secessionist and ardently devoted to the Southern cause. Circumstances of an imperious nature, which it is unnecessary to relate here, had prevented him from taking service with the gallant army that had fought the disastrous campaigns ending with the fall of Corinth, and he chafed under the inglorious restraint, longing for the release of his energies, the larger life of the soldier, the opportunity for distinction. That opportunity, he felt, would come, as it comes to all in wartime. Meanwhile he did what he could. No service was too humble for him to perform in aid of the South, no adventure too perilous for him to undertake if consistent with the character of a civilian who was at heart a soldier, and who in good faith and without too much qualification assented to at least a part of the frankly villainous dictum that all is fair in love and war.

One evening while Farquhar and his wife were sitting on a rustic bench near the entrance to his grounds, a mere grey-clad soldier rode up to the gate and asked for a drink of water. Mrs Farquhar was only too happy to serve him with her own white hands. While she was fetching the water her husband approached the dusty horseman and inquired eagerly for news from the front.

"The Yanks are repairing the railroads," said the man, "and are getting ready for another advance. They have reached the Owl Creek bridge, put it in order and built a stockade on the north bank. The commandant has issued an order, which is posted everywhere, declaring that any civilian caught interfer-

39

ing with the railroad, its bridges, tunnels or trains will be summarily hanged. I saw the order."

"How far is it to Owl Creek bridge?" Farquhar asked.

"About thirty miles."

"Is there no force on this side of the creek?"

"Only a picket post half a mile out, on the railroad, and a single sentinel at this end of the ridge."

"Suppose a man—a civilian and student of hanging—should elude the picket post and perhaps get the better of the sentinel," said Farquhar, smiling, "what could he accomplish?"

The soldier reflected. "I was there a month ago," he replied. "I observed that the flood of last winter had lodged a great quantity of driftwood against the wooden pier at this end of the bridge. It is now dry and would burn like tow."

The lady had now brought the water, which the soldier drank. He thanked her ceremoniously, bowed to her husband and rode away. An hour later, after nightfall, he repassed the plantation, going northward in the direction from which he had come. He was a Federal scout.

As Peyton Farquhar fell straight downward through the bridge he lost consciousness and was as one already dead. From this state he was awakened—ages later, it seemed to him—by the pain of a sharp pressure upon his throat, followed by a sense of suffocation. Keen, poignant agonies seemed to shoot from his neck downward through every fibre of his body and limbs. These pains appeared to flash along well-defined lines of ramification and to beat with an inconceivably rapid periodicity. They seemed like streams of pulsating fire heating him to an intolerable temperature. As to his head, he was conscious of nothing but a feeling of fullness—of congestion. These sensations were unaccompanied by thought. The intellectual part of his nature was already effaced; he had power only to feel, and feeling was torment. He was conscious of motion. Encompassed in a luminous cloud, of which he was now merely the fiery heart, without material substance, he swung through unthinkable arcs of oscillation, like a vast pendulum. Then all at once, with terrible suddenness, the light about him shot upward with the noise of a loud splash; a frightful roaring was in his ears, and all was cold and dark. The power of thought was restored; he knew that the rope had broken and he had fallen into the stream. There was no additional strangulation; the noose about his neck was already suffocating him and kept the water from his lungs. To die of hanging at the bottom of a river!—the idea seemed to him ludicrous. He opened his eyes in the darkness and saw above him a gleam of light, but how distant, how inaccessible! He was still sinking, for the light became fainter and fainter until it was a mere glimmer. Then it began to grow and brighten, and he knew that he was rising toward the surface—knew it with reluctance, for he was now very comfortable. "To be hanged and drowned," he thought, "that is not so bad; but I do no wish to be shot. No; I will not be shot; that is not fair."

He was not conscious of an effort, but a sharp pain in his wrist apprised him that he was trying to free his hands. He gave the struggle his attention, as an idler might observe the feat of a juggler, without interest in the outcome. What spendid effort!—what magnificent, what superhuman strength! Ah, that was a fine endeavour! Bravo! The cord fell away; his arms parted and floated upward, the hands dimly seen on each side in the growing light. He watched them with a new interest as first one and then the other pounced upon the noose at his neck. They tore it away and thrust it fiercely aside, its undulations resembling those of a water-snake. "Put it back, put it back!" He thought he shouted these words to his hands, for the undoing of the noose had been succeeded by the direst pain that he had yet experienced. His neck ached horribly; his brain was on fire; his heart, which had been fluttering faintly, gave a great leap, trying to force itself out at his mouth. His whole body was racked and wrenched with an insupportable anguish! But his disobedient hands gave no heed to the command. They beat the water vigorously with quick, downward strokes, forcing him to the surface. He felt his head emerge; his eyes were blinded by the sunlight; his chest expanded convulsively, and with a supreme and crowning agony his lungs engulfed a great draught of air, which instantly he expelled in a shriek!

He was now in full possession of his physical senses. They were, indeed, preternaturally keen and alert. Something in the awful disturbance of his organic system had so exalted and refined them that they made record of things never before perceived. He felt the ripples upon his face and heard their separate sounds as they struck. He looked at the forest on the bank of the stream, saw the individual trees, the leaves and the veining of each leaf—saw the insects upon them: the locusts, the brilliant-bodied flies, the grey spiders stretching their webs from twig to twig. He noted the prismatic colours in all the dewdrops upon a million blades of grass. The humming of the gnats that danced above the eddies of the stream, the beating of the dragonflies' wings, the strokes of the water-spiders' legs, like oars which had lifted their boat—all these made audible music. A fish slid along beneath his eyes and he heard the rush of its body parting the water.

He had come to the surface facing down the stream; in a moment the visible world seemed to wheel slowly round, himself the pivotal point, and he saw the bridge, the fort, the soldiers upon the bridge, the captain, the sergeant, the two privates, his executioners. They were in silhouette against the blue sky. They shouted and gesticulated, pointing at him. The captain had drawn his pistol, but did not fire; the others were unarmed. Their movements were grotesque and horrible, their forms gigantic.

Suddenly he heard a sharp report and something struck the water smartly within a few inches of his head, spattering his face with spray. He heard a second report, and saw one of the sentinels with his rifle at his shoulder, a light cloud of blue smoke rising from the muzzle. The man in the water saw the eye of the man on the bridge gazing into his own through the sights of the rifle. He observed that it was a grey eye and remembered having read that grey eyes were keenest, and that all famous marksmen had them. Nevertheless, this one had missed.

42

A counter-swirl had caught Farquhar and turned him half round; he was again looking into the forest on the bank opposite the fort. The sound of a clear, high voice in a monotonous sing-song now rang out behind him and came across the water with a distinctness that pierced and subdued all other sounds, even the beating of the ripples in his ears. Although no soldier, he had frequented camps enough to know the dread significance of that deliberate, drawling, aspirated chant; the lieutenant on shore was taking a part in the morning's work. How coldly and pitilessly—with what an even, calm intonation, presaging, and enforcing tranquillity in the men—with what accurately measured intervals fell those cruel words:

"Attention, company! . . . Shoulder arms! . . . Ready! . . . Aim! . . . Fire!"

Farquhar dived—dived as deeply as he could. The water roared in his ears like the voice of Niagara, yet he heard the dulled thunder of the volley and, rising again toward the surface, met shining bits of metal, singularly flattened, oscillating slowly downward. Some of them touched him on the face and hands, then fell away, continuing their descent. One lodged between his collar and neck; it was uncomfortably warm and he snatched it out.

As he rose to the surface, gasping for breath, he saw that he had been a long time under water; he was perceptibly farther down stream—nearer to safety. The soldiers had almost finished reloading; the metal ramrods flashed all at once in the sunshine as they were drawn from the barrels, turned in the air, and thrust into their sockets. The two sentinels fired again, independently, and ineffectually.

The hunted man saw all this over his shoulder; he was now swimming vigorously with the current. His brain was as energetic as his arms and legs; he thought with the rapidity of lightning.

"The officer," he reasoned, "will not make that martinet's error a second time. It is easy to dodge a volley as a single shot. He has probably already given the command to fire at will. God help me, I cannot dodge them all!"

An appalling splash within two yards of him was followed by a loud rushing sound, *diminuendo*, which seemed to travel back through the air to the fort and died in an explosion which stirred the very river to its deeps! A rising sheet of water curved over him, fell down upon him, blinded him, strangled him! The cannon had taken a hand in the game. As he shook his head free from the commotion of the smitten water he heard the deflected shot humming through the air ahead, and in an instant it was cracking and smashing the branches in the forest beyond.

"They will not do that again," he thought; "the next time they will use a charge of grape. I must keep my eye upon the gun; the smoke will apprise me—the report arrives too late; it lags behind the missile. That is a good gun."

Suddenly he felt himself whirled round and round—spinning like a top. The water, the banks, the forests, the now distant bridge, fort and men—all were mingled and blurred. Objects were represented by their colours only; circular horizontal streaks of colour—that was all he saw. He had been caught in a vortex and was being whirled on with a velocity of advance and gyration that made him giddy and sick. In a few moments he was flung upon the gravel at the foot of the left bank of the stream— the southern bank—and behind a projecting point which concealed him from his enemies. The sudden arrest of his motion, the abrasion of one of his hands on the gravel, restored him, and he wept with delight. He dug his fingers into the sand, threw it over himself in handfuls and audibly blessed it. It looked like diamonds, rubies, emeralds; he could think of nothing beautiful which it did not resemble. The trees upon the bank were giant garden plants; he noted a definite order in their arrangement, inhaled the fragrance of their blooms. A strange, roseate light shone through the spaces among their trunks and the wind made in their branches the music of aeolian harps. He had no wish to make perfect his escape—was content to remain in that enchanting spot until retaken.

A whizz and rattle of grapeshot among the branches high above his head roused him from his dream. The baffled cannoneer had fired him a random farewell. He sprang to his feet, rushed up the sloping bank, and plunged into the forest.

All that day he travelled, laying his course by the rounding sun. The forest seemed interminable; nowhere did he discover a break in it, not even a woodman's road. He had not known that he lived in so wild a region. There was something uncanny in the revelation.

By nightfall he was fatigued, footsore, famished. The thought of his wife and children urged him on. At last he found a road which led him in what he knew to be the right direction. It was as wide and straight as a city street, yet it seemed untravelled. No fields bordered it, no dwelling anywhere. Not so much as the barking of a dog suggested human habitation. The black bodies of the trees formed a straight wall on both sides, terminating on the horizon in a point, like a diagram in a lesson in perspective. Overhead, as he looked up through this rift in the wood, shone great golden stars looking unfamiliar and grouped in strange constellations. He was sure they were arranged in some order which had a secret and malign significance. The wood on either side was full of singular noises, among which—once, twice, and again—he distinctly heard whispers in an unknown tongue.

His neck was in pain and lifting his hand to it he found it horribly swollen. he knew that it had a circle of black where the rope had bruised it. His eyes felt congested; he could no longer close them. His tongue was swollen with thirst; he relieved its fever by thrusting it forward from between his teeth into the cold air. How softly the turf had carpeted the untravelled avenue—he could no longer feel the roadway beneath his feet!

Doubtless, despite his suffering, he had fallen asleep while walking, for now he sees another scene—perhaps he has merely recovered from a delirium. He stands at the gate of his own home. All is as he left it, and all bright and beautiful in the morning sunshine. He must have travelled the entire night. As he pushes open the gate and passes up the wide white walk, he sees a flutter of female garments; his wife, looking fresh and cool and sweet, steps down from the veranda to meet him. At the bottom

45

"His wife, looking fresh and cool and sweet, steps
down from the verandah to meet him."

of the steps she stands waiting, with a smile of ineffable joy, an attitude of matchless grace and dignity. Ah, how beautiful she is! He springs forward with extended arms. As he is about to clasp her he feels a stunning blow upon the back of the neck; a blinding white light blazes all about him with a sound like the shock of a cannon—then all is darkness and silence!

Peyton Farquhar was dead; his body, with a broken neck, swung gently from side to side beneath the timbers of the Owl Creek bridge.

The Coming of the Tiger

by J. S. LEE

In 1894, James Lee, then twenty-two years old, became mechanical engineer in a mining settlement on the north-eastern frontier of India. This story is of one the many exciting adventures which befell him.

I was in grand form; I found life very interesting, for there was plenty of variety here.

I have seen a man-eater, a tiger. Not only that, but I have smelt its foul breath on my face, and have almost felt its claws when reaching for me, within a few inches of my body. Yet I am still alive, but the memory of it will live with me for ever. Those hours of fear were torture far more acute than any pain; a mental torture which I never before realised was possible to be produced by fear. Yes, believe me, fear can be more agonising than bodily pain.

I was sleeping in my bed when I was awakened in the early hours of the morning by a coolie standing under my window, calling, "Sahib! Sahib!"

As soon as I awakened, I got up and went to the open window—a window which contained no glass; only a wooden-louvred shutter.

"Sahib, *harkul bund hai,*" said the coolie, meaning, "The fan has stopped."

This was a very serious matter. I knew that there were more than a hundred men and women working underground on the night shift, and soon the air underground would be unbreatheable, and work would have to stop. The fan must be got going at once. I got up and dressed quickly, meanwhile sending the coolie for one of my fitters, who had a hut just below my compound.

Luckai, the fitter, an old man something like an Egyptian mummy in appearance, came up to my compound, carrying a hurricane lamp and a large pipe wrench, while the coolie fireman followed carrying some tools.

It was no joke, really, for we had to walk about half a mile through the jungle before we got to the fan, which was situated in an isolated spot, right in the heart of the jungle, and high up the hillside.

I was always scared on this trip at night-time, and I had made it a few times under similar conditions; the fan had a habit of stopping sometimes at night. It might be the feed pump of the boiler which had gone wrong, or perhaps the coolie had allowed the water to get out of sight in the gauge glass, when he would get scared, draw the fire, and come down for a fitter.

I was scared because the jungle was known to be infested by tigers and leopards, and many natives had been killed at one time or another in the district.

As we walked along the winding path up the side of the hill, with thick jungle on either side, the old man was fairly trembling, and muttering to himself: "Khun roj Bargh kyh-ager," which means literally, "Some day tiger eat".

The coolie was the only one of us who appeared not to be afraid, but then perhaps he had no imagination; he was a poor specimen of humanity: naked, with the exception of a loin-cloth, and coal black, with spindle legs and big feet; and his face and arms were covered with syphilitic sores.

I would certainly have taken my rifle with me, but it would not have been much protection at night-time.

A tiger could spring out on us before I could use it, or a leopard could jump down on us out of a tree as we passed underneath;

besides, I knew that I would come in for a good deal of chaff from the other Europeans. I carried a hunting knife only.

Although I reckoned that the chances of us meeting a tiger were about 100 to 1 against, this did not seem to help much.

Arrived at the spot I proceeded to investigate.

The place was a levelled and cleared portion of the hillside towering above us. Here there was a horizontal engine and a large vertical boiler, standing on a massive concrete foundation, and driving, by means of a leather belt, the fan, which was built in the hillside. In front of me the jungle sloped away steeply down to the valley below.

The boiler fire was out, and the steam had fallen to a few pounds' pressure, and steam and water were leaking into the furnace.

I knew that there was a tube leaking, probably the uptake tube. It was a very old boiler and all I could do was to make a temporary repair.

Leaving Lukai and the coolie to blow off the water and take off the manhole cover, I proceeded down the hill by a different route to the mine entrance, to see the foreman miner, and tell him to withdraw the coolies; the repair would take the rest of the night to make.

By the time I got back, I found that they had got the water blown off, and the manhole opened, leaving an opening into the boiler several feet above the ground.

They had a ladder placed against the boiler, and Lukai was on the domed roof, taking off the chimney, while the coolie was down below raking out the ashes, and taking out the fire-bars, so that I could stand upright when inside the furnace. The interior was still hot, so we started to partly fill the boiler with cold water as high as the furnace crown, on which we would have to stand when inside the steam space.

Although we had thrown buckets of cold water all round inside the furnace door, the interior was also fairly hot and stifling when I crept inside with a small lamp.

Meanwhile Lukai got into the boiler through the manhole

overhead, and between us we located the leak. As I expected, it was a small leak through the uptake tube. It had worn thin just there. Really it was dangerous, but as it would take a week to get another boiler up, and we could not stop the mine working, I had to patch it up as quickly as I could.

I next got in the manhole beside Lukai, and while he held the lamp, I punched a round chisel or drift through the leak until I had made a round hole large enough for a half-inch bolt to pass through.

This done, we got outside and found two pieces of plate of about two inches square, with a hole through the centre of each, for the bolt to pass through. These plates or washers were slightly curved, so as to fit the tube.

Wrapping the neck of the bolt with spunyarn, and covering it with red and white lead, I threaded on a plate, first passing the second piece of plate up to Lukai, who had climbed into the manhole.

Again getting inside the firedoor, I reached up the tube, and pushed the bolt through the hole, until the plate, well-covered with lead and spunyarn, was pressing firmly against the tube.

Lukai now threaded his piece of plate on to the bolt from the other side of the tube, first well leading and wrapping it; and all that now required to be done was for him to put on the nut and tighten up, so that the leak would be tightly gripped by the plates, inside and outside.

Just then I heard the coolie scream, and saw his legs and feet scampering up the ladder.

He was now on top of the boiler shouting, "Bargh" ("tiger").

The sudden realisation of my position now struck me for the first time. I was trapped like a rat in a trap. I was on the ground level, and there was an open hole into the chamber.

Could the tiger reach me with its claws, through the open door? I felt that it could, and I knew then real fear, such as few people ever experience.

Thoughts raced through my brain, quickly following one another. I thought of our relative positions.

51

The coolie was on top of the boiler, high up out of reach of the tiger, and therefore safe. Lukai was inside the boiler, and the only opening into this part was the manhole, and this was several feet above the ground. He was fairly safe, I thought, because the tiger could not climb up the smooth steel side. My position was the only one which was dangerous. I could now hear it moving about outside, and once or twice I caught a glimpse of its stripes, as it passed the door opening, because the night was not dark, the stars were shining above us.

The creature evidently had not yet discovered my presence, and was concentrating its attention on the coolie above.

It moved in silence, and both Lukai and the coolie were now silent.

Suddenly, with a terrible snarl, it sprang upwards, and I could hear its claws rasping on the steel plate as it slipped back. Its rage and snarls were now horrible, and all the time I was pressing myself back against the far side of the boiler as hard as I could.

Could it reach me when it discovered my presence?

I measured the distance with my eye, and I felt more hopeful.

Suddenly the snarling stopped, and I saw its head at the opening. It had found me.

First it tried to force itself through the door, but it could only get its head through, and its fangs soon were snapping within a couple of feet of my body. Its breath came in horrid, foul gusts, filling the chamber with a sickening odour, and its roars inside the confined space were enough to hurt my ear-drums, while its eyes were glaring into mine.

I stood there fascinated with horror.

I now knew that it could not reach me that way, but would it start reaching in with its claws? My imagination now began to visualise its claws reaching me, and speculating as to what part of me it would rip up first. The constriction on my heart had almost become like a physical pain. Just then I heard something strike the boiler plate with a loud clang. Lukai had thrown his hammer. Of course. How foolish of me! I had forgotten my hunting knife,

"First it tried to force itself through the door, but it could only get its head through ..."

which was in my belt. I would wait until the tiger put its head in again, and then try and jab the blade through its eye into the brain.

Now it was reaching for me with its paw through the door opening, and its claws came within a few inches of my body, opening and shutting in a horrible manner. It could not reach me, but I knew that if it had the intelligence of a human being, it would reach in sideways, and then all would soon be over.

It was too dangerous to try and slash its paw; besides, it would do little good. I would wait.

Again it had got its head in the opening and I raised my knife, but found that its teeth followed my hand, and it was risky to strike, because it was snapping all the time. Its top lip was lifted, exposing fangs which seemed enormous, and its whiskers were trembling with rage.

Then I struck with all the suddenness I was capable of. I had missed, and the knife only slashed down its nose, because its head had moved.

Quickly the tiger backed out with a roar. Its rage now was so terrible that it even bit at the plate of the door opening. It was behaving outside like a rampaging demon; lashing its tail and sometimes springing up at the coolie, who had now recovered his courage when he found himself beyond reach. Both he and Lukai were spitting and hissing and hurling abuse at it.

Once on its upward spring it got its paw in the manhole door opening, and hung there a minute while the rest of its claws were slipping and rasping on the steel plates of the boiler side. Then Lukai brought his spanner down with all his force on its paw, nearly cutting it through on the sharp edge of the door opening.

Now the creature was almost insane with rage. It had first been hit by Lukai on the back with a hammer, then its nose had been split by my knife, and lastly its paw had been nearly cut off by the last blow.

Presently it put its head in the fire-door again, and, following Lukai's example, I struck it a heavy blow on the nose with my large hammer.

"I struck it a heavy blow on the nose with my large hammer."

Now a tiger's nose is a very tender and sensitive spot, and it is intended to be so, because its whiskers have to guide it through the thick undergrowth in the dark, and it feels the touch of any obstruction first through these, and then through its nose; consequently the pain must have been extremely acute, judging by the noise it made. It then bounded off into the jungle.

However, none of us ventured to leave our refuge before it was broad daylight, and in the meantime we completed the work.

Solomon's Treasure Chamber

by H. R. RIDER HAGGARD

The fabulous mines of King Solomon lie deep in the heart of Africa. Following an old map drawn by an explorer, Jose da Silvestra, the hunter, Allan Quatermain (nicknamed Macumazahn), and his companions Captain Good (nicknamed Bougwan) and Sir Henry Curtis, reach the lost land of Kukuana. After many adventures and dangers they overthrow the cruel king Twala. Now, led by his evil witch-finder Gagool, they enter the mines. They stop, amazed, in the chamber of Death where they see the petrified bodies of the kings of the Kukuanas made into stalactites by the perpetual dripping of the water from the roof.

While we were engaged in recovering from our fright, and in examining the grisly wonders of the Place of Death, Gagool had been differently occupied. Somehow or other—for she was marvellously active when she chose—she had scrambled on to the great table, and made her way to where our departed friend Twala was placed under the drip, to see, suggested Good, how he was "pickling", or for some dark purpose of her own. Then she hobbled back, stopping now and again to address a remark, the tenor of which I could not catch, to one or other of the shrouded forms, just as you or I might greet an old acquaintance. Having gone through this mysterious and horrible ceremony, she squatted herself down on the table immediately under the

57

"*The Palace of Death.*"

White Death, and began, so far as I could make out, to offer up prayers to it. The spectacle of this wicked old creature pouring out supplications—evil ones, no doubt—to the arch enemy of mankind, was so uncanny that it caused us to hasten our inspection.

"Now, Gagool," said I, in a low voice—somehow one did not dare to speak above a whisper in that place—"lead us to the chamber."

The old creature promptly scrambled down off the table.

"My lords are not afraid?" she said, leering up into my face.

"Lead on."

"Good, my lords!" and she hobbled round to the back of the great Death. "Here is the chamber; let my lords light the lamp, and enter," and she placed the gourd full of oil upon the floor, and leaned herself against the side of the cave. I took out a match, of which we had still a few in a box, and lit a rush wick, and then looked for the doorway, but there was nothing before us except the solid rock. Gagool grinned. "The way is there, my lords. *Ha! ha! ha!*"

"Do not jest with us," I said sternly.

"I jest not, my lords. See!" and she pointed at the rock.

As she did so, on holding up the lamp we perceived that a mass of stone was rising slowly from the floor and vanishing into the rock above, where doubtless there is a cavity prepared to receive it. The mass was of the width of a good-sized door, about ten feet high and not less than five feet thick. It must have weighed at least twenty or thirty tons, and was clearly moved upon some simple balance principle of counterweights, probably the same as that by which the opening and shutting of an ordinary modern window is arranged. How the principle was set in motion, of course none of us saw; Gagool was careful to avoid this, but I have little doubt that there was some very simple lever, which was moved ever so little by pressure on a secret spot, thereby throwing additional weight on to the hidden counterbalances, and causing the whole mass to be lifted from the ground.

Very slowly and gently the great stone raised itself, until at last it had vanished altogether, and a dark hole presented itself to us in the place which the door had filled.

Our excitement was so intense, as we saw the way to Solomon's treasure chamber thrown open at last, that I for one began to tremble and shake. Would it prove a hoax after all? I wondered, or was old da Silvestra right, and were there vast hoards of wealth stored in that dark place, hoards which would make us the richest men in the whole world? We should know in a minute or two.

"Enter, white men from the Stars," said Gagool, advancing into the doorway; "but first hear your servant, Gagool the old. The bright stones that ye will see were dug out of the pit over which the Silent Ones are set, and stored, here, I know not by whom. But once has this place been entered since the time that those who stored the stones departed in haste, leaving them behind. The report of the treasure went down indeed among the people who lived in the country from age to age, but none knew where the chamber was, nor the secret of the door. But it happened that a white man reached this country from over the mountains-perchance he too came 'from the Stars'—and was well received by the king of that day. He it is who sits yonder," and she pointed to the fifth king at the table of the Dead. "And it came to pass that he and a woman of the country who was with him journeyed to this place, and that by chance the woman learnt the secret of the door—a thousand years might ye search, but ye should never find it. Then the white man entered with the woman and found the stones, and filled with stones the skin of a small goat, which the woman had with her to hold food. And as he was going from the chamber he took up one more stone, a large one, and held it in his hand." Here she paused.

"Well," I asked, breathless with interest as we all were, "what happened to da Silvestra?"

The old hag started at the mention of the name.

"How knowest thou the dead man's name?" she asked sharply; and then, without waiting for an answer, went on—

"None know what happened; but it came about that the white

60

man was frightened, for he flung down the goat-skin, with the stones, and fled out with only the one stone in his hand, and that the king took, and it is the stone which thou, Macumazahn, didst take from Twala's brow."

"Have none entered here since?" I asked, peering again down the dark passage.

"None, my lords. Only the secret of the door has been kept, and every king has opened it, though he has not entered. There is a saying, that those who enter there will die within a moon, even as the white man died in the cave upon the mountain, where ye found him, Macumazahn, and therefore the kings do not enter. *Ha! ha!* mine are true words."

Our eyes met as she said it, and I turned sick and cold. How did the old hag know all these things?

"Enter, my lords. If I speak truth, the goat-skin with the stones will lie upon the floor; and if there is truth as to whether it is death to enter here, that will ye learn afterwards. *Ha! ha! ha!*" and she hobbled through the doorway, bearing the light with her; but I confess that once more I hesitated about following.

"Oh, confound it all!" said Good; "here goes. I am not going to be frightened by that old devil!" and followed by Foulata, who, however, evidently did not at all like the business, for she was shivering with fear, he plunged into the passage after Gagool —an example which we quickly followed.

A few yards down the passage, in the narrow way hewn out of the living rock, Gagool had paused, and was waiting for us.

"See, my lords," she said, holding the light before her, "those who stored the treasure here fled in haste, and bethought them to guard against any who should find the secret of the door, but had not the time," and she pointed to large square blocks of stone, which, to the height of two courses (about two feet three), had been placed across the passage with a view to walling it up. Along the side of the passage were similar blocks ready for use, and, most curious of all, a heap of mortar and a couple of trowels, which tools, so far as we had time to examine them, appeared to be of a similar shape and make to those used by workmen to this day.

Here Foulata, who had been in a state of great fear and agitation throughout, said that she felt faint and could go no farther, but would wait there. Accordingly we set her down on the unfinished wall, placing the basket of provisions by her side, and left her to recover.

Following the passage for about fifteen paces farther, we came suddenly to an elaborately painted wooden door. It was standing wide open. Whoever was last there had either not found the time, or had forgotten, to shut it.

Across the threshold of this door lay a skin bag, formed of a goatskin, that appeared to be full of pebbles!

"*Hee! hee!* white men," sniggered Gagool, as the light from the lamp fell upon it. "What did I tell you, that the white man who came here fled in haste, and dropped the woman's bag—behold it!"

Good stooped down and lifted it. It was heavy and jingled.

"By Jove! I believe it's full of diamonds," he said, in an awed whisper; and, indeed, the idea of a small goat-skin full of diamonds is enough to awe anybody.

"Go on," said Henry impatiently. "Here, old lady, give me the lamp," and, taking it from Gagool's hand, he stepped through the doorway and held it high above his head.

We pressed in after him, forgetful for the moment of the bag of diamonds, and found ourselves in Solomon's treasure chamber.

At first, all that the somewhat faint light given by the lamp revealed was a room hewn out of the living rock, and apparently not more than ten feet square. Next there came into sight, stored one on the other to the arch of the roof, a splendid collection of elephant-tusks. How many of them there were we did not know, for of course we could not see to what depth they went back, but there could not have been less than the ends of four or five hundred tusks of the first quality visible to our eyes. There alone was enough ivory before us to make a man wealthy for life. Perhaps, I thought, it was from this very store that Solomon drew the raw

62

material for his "great throne of ivory", of which "there was not the like made in any kingdom."

On the opposite side of the chamber were about a score of wooden boxes, something like Martini-Henry ammunition boxes, only rather larger, and painted red.

"There are the diamonds," cried I, "bring the light."

Sir Henry did so, holding it close to the top box, of which the lid, rendered rotten by time even in that dry place, appeared to have been smashed in, probably by da Silvestra himself. Pushing my hand through the hole in the lid I drew it out full, not of diamonds, but of gold pieces, of a shape that none of us had seen before, and with what looked like Hebrew characters stamped upon them.

"Ah!" I said, replacing the coin, "we shan't go back empty-handed, anyhow. There must be a couple of thousand pieces in each box, and there are eighteen boxes. I suppose this was the money to pay the workmen and merchants."

"Well," put in Good, "I think that is the lot; I don't see any diamonds, unless the old Portuguee put them all into his bag."

"Let my lords look yonder where it is darkest, if they would find the stones," said Gagool, interpreting our looks. "There my lords will find a nook, and three stone chests in the nook, two sealed and one open."

Before translating this to Sir Henry, who carried the light, I could not resist asking how she knew these things, if no one had entered the place since the white man, generations ago.

"Ah, Macumazahn, the watcher by night," was the mocking answer, "ye who live in the stars, do ye not know that some have eyes which can see through rock? *Ha! ha! ha!*"

"Look in that corner, Curtis," I said, indicating the spot Gagool had pointed out.

"Hullo, you fellows," he cried, "here's a recess. Great heavens! see here."

We hurried up to where he was standing in a nook, shaped something like a small bow window. Against the wall of this

63

recess were placed three stone chests, each about two feet square. Two were fitted with stone lids, the lid of the third rested against the side of the chest, which was open.

"*See!*" he repeated hoarsely, holding a lamp over the open chest. We looked, and for a moment could make nothing out, on account of a silvery sheen that dazzled us. When our eyes grew used to it we saw that the chest was three parts full of uncut diamonds, most of them of considerable size. Stooping, I picked some up. Yes, there was no doubt of it, there was the unmistakable soapy feel about them.

I fairly gasped as I dropped them.

"We are the richest men in the whole world," I said. "Monte Cristo was a fool to us."

"We shall flood the market with diamonds," said Good.

"Got to get them there first," suggested Sir Henry.

We stood still with pale faces and stared at each other, the lantern in the middle and the glimmering gems below, as though we were conspirators about to commit a crime, instead of being, as we thought, the most fortunate men on earth.

"*Hee! hee! hee!*" cackled old Gagool behind us, as she flitted about like a vampire bat. "There are the bright stones ye love, white men, as many as ye will; take them, run them through your fingers, *eat* of them, *hee! hee!*, *drink* of them, *ha! ha!*"

At that moment there was something so ridiculous to my mind in the idea of eating and drinking diamonds, that I began to laugh outrageously, an example which the others followed, without knowing why. There we stood and shrieked with laughter over the gems that were ours, which had been found for *us* thousands of years ago by the patient delvers in the great hole yonder, and stored for *us* by Solomon's long-dead overseer, whose name, perchance, was written in the characters stamped on the faded wax that yet adhered to the lids of the chests. Solomon never got them, nor David, nor da Silvestra, nor anybody else. *We* had got them; there before us were millions of pounds' worth of diamonds, and thousands of pounds' worth of gold and ivory only waiting to be taken away.

"Pushing my hand through the hole in the lid I drew it out full, not of diamonds, but of gold pieces."

Suddenly the fit passed off, and we stopped laughing.

"Open the other chests, white men," croaked Gagool, "there are surely more therein. Take your fill, white lords! *Ha! ha!* take your fill."

Thus adjured, we set to work to pull up the stone lids on the other two, first—not without a feeling of sacrilege—breaking the seals that fastened them.

Hoorah! they were full too, full to the brim; at least the second one was; no wretched da Silvestra had been filling goat-skins out of that. As for the third chest, it was only about a fourth full, but the stones were all picked ones; none less than twenty carats, and some of them as large as pigeon-eggs. A good many of these bigger ones, however, we could see by holding them up to the light, were a little yellow, "off coloured", as they call it at Kimberley.

What we did *not* see, however, was the look of fearful malevolence that old Gagool favoured us with as she crept, crept like a snake, out of the treasure chamber and down the passage towards the door of solid rock.

Hark! Cry upon cry comes ringing up the vaulted path. It is Foulata's voice!

"Oh, Bougwan! help! help! the stone falls!"

"Leave go, girl! Then ..."

"Help! help! she has stabbed me!"

By now we are running down the passage, and this is what the light from the lamp shows us. The door of rock is closing down slowly; it is not three feet from the floor. Near it struggle Foulata and Gagool. The red blood of the former runs to her knee, but still the brave girl holds the old witch, who fights like a wild cat. Ah! she is free! Foulata falls, and Gagool throws herself on the ground, to twist like a snake through the crack of the closing stone. She is under—ah! God! too late! too late! The stone nips her, and she yells in agony. Down, down, it comes, all the thirty tons of it, slowly pressing her old body against the rock below. Shriek upon shriek, such as we never heard, then a long sickening

66

"Down, down it comes, all the thirty tons of it, slowly pressing her old body against the rock below."

crunch, and the door was shut, just as, rushing down the passage, we hurled ourselves against it.

It was all done in four seconds.

Then we turned to Foulata. The poor girl was stabbed in the body, and I saw that she could not live long.

"Ah! Bougwan, I die!" gasped the beautiful creature. "She crept out—Gagool; I did not see her, I was faint—and the door began to fall. Then she came back, and was looking up the path—I saw her come in through the slowly falling door, and caught her and held her, and she stabbed me, and I *die*, Bougwan!"

"Poor girl! poor girl!" Good cried; and then, as he could do nothing else, he fell to kissing her.

"Bougwan," she said, after a pause, "is Macumazahn there? It grows so dark, I cannot see."

"Here I am, Foulata."

"Macumazahn, be my tongue for a moment, I pray thee, for Bougwan cannot understand me, and before I go into the darkness I would speak a word."

"Say on, Foulata, I will render it."

"Say to my lord, Bougwan, that—I love him, and that I am glad to die because I know that he cannot cumber his life with such as I am, for the sun may not mate with the darkness, nor the white with the black.

"Say that, since I saw him, at times I have felt as though there were a bird in my bosom, which would one day fly hence and sing elsewhere. Even now, though I cannot lift my hand, and my brain grows cold, I do not feel as though my heart were dying; it is so full of love that it could live a thousand years, and yet be young. Say that if I live again, mayhap I shall see him in the Stars, and that—I will search them all, though perchance there I should still be black and he would—still be white. Say—nay, Macumazahn, say no more, save that I love——Oh, hold me closer, Bougwan, I cannot feel thine arms—*oh! oh!*"

"She is dead—she is dead!" exclaimed Good, rising in grief, the tears running down his honest face.

"You need not let that trouble you, old fellow," said Sir Henry.

"Eh?" said Good; "what do you mean?"

"I mean that you will soon be in a position to join her. *Man, don't you see that we are buried alive?*"

Until Sir Henry uttered these words I do not think that the full horror of what had happened had come home to us, preoccupied as we were with the sight of poor Foulata's end, but now we understood. The ponderous mass of rock had closed, probably for ever, for the only brain which knew its secret was crushed to powder beneath it. This was a door that none could hope to force with anything short of dynamite in large quantities. And we were the wrong side of it!

For a few minutes we stood horrified there over the corpse of Foulata. All the manhood seemed to have gone out of us. The first shock of this idea of the slow and miserable end that awaited us was overpowering. We saw it all now; that fiend Gagool had planned this snare for us from the first. It must have been just the jest that her evil mind would have rejoiced in, the idea of the three white men, whom, for some reason of her own, she had always hated, slowly perishing of thirst and hunger in the company of the treasure they had coveted. Now I saw the point of that sneer of hers about eating and drinking the diamonds. Perhaps somebody had tried to serve the poor old Dom in the same way, when he abandoned the skin full of jewels.

"This will never do," said Sir Henry hoarsely; "the lamp will soon go out. Let us see if we can find the spring that works the rock."

We sprang forward with desperate energy, and, standing in a bloody ooze, began to feel up and down the door and the sides of the passage. But no knob or spring could we discover.

"Depend on it," I said, "it does not work from the inside; if it did, Gagool would not have risked trying to crawl underneath the stone. It was the knowledge of this that made her try to escape at all hazards, curse her."

"At all events," said Sir Henry, with a hard little laugh, "retribution was swift; hers was almost as awful an end as ours is

69

likely to be. We can do nothing with the door; let us go back to the treasure room."

We turned and went, and as we passed it I perceived by the unfinished wall across the passage the basket of food which poor Foulata had carried. I took it up, and brought it with me to the accursed treasure chamber that was to be our grave. Then we returned and reverently bore in Foulata's corpse, laying it on the floor by the boxes of coins.

Next we seated ourselves, leaning our backs against the three stone chests of priceless treasure.

"Let us divide the food," said Sir Henry, "so as to make it last as long as possible." Accordingly we did so. It would, we reckoned, make four infinitesimally small meals for each of us, enough, say, to support life for a couple of days. Besides the "biltong" or dried game-flesh, there were two goords of water, each holding about a quart.

"Now," said Sir Henry grimly, "let us eat and drink, for tomorrow we die."

We ate a small portion of the "biltong" and drank a sip of water. Needless to say, we had but little appetite, though we were sadly in need of food, and felt better after swallowing it. Then we got up and made a systematic examination of the walls of our prison-house, in the faint hope of finding some means of exit, sounding them and the floor carefully.

There was none. It was not probable that there would be any to a treasure chamber.

The lamp began to burn dim. The fat was nearly exhausted.

"Quatermain," said Sir Henry, "what is the time—your watch goes?"

I drew it out and looked at it. It was six o'clock; we had entered the cave at eleven.

"Infadoos will miss us," I suggested. "If we do not return tonight he will search for us in the morning, Curtis."

"He may search in vain. He does not know the secret of the door nor even where it is. No living person knew it yesterday, except Gagool. To-day no one knows it. Even if he found the door he could not break it down. All the Kukuana army could not break through five feet of living rock. My friends, I see nothing for it but to bow ourselves to the will of the Almighty. The search for treasure has brought many to a bad end; we shall go to swell their number."

The lamp grew dimmer yet.

Presently it flared up and showed the whole scene in strong relief, the great mass of white tusks, the boxes of gold, the corpse of poor Foulata stretched before them, the goat-skin full of treasure, the dim glimmer of the diamonds, and the wild, wan faces of us three white men seated there awaiting death by starvation.

Then the flame sank and expired.

I can give no adequate description of the horrors of the night which followed. Mercifully they were to some extent mitigated by sleep, for even in such a position as ours wearied nature will sometimes assert herself. But I, at any rate, found it impossible to sleep much. Putting aside the terrifying thought of our impending doom—for the bravest man on earth might well quail from such a fate as awaited us, and I never made any pretensions to be brave—the *silence* itself was too great to allow of it. Reader, you may have lain awake at night and thought the silence oppressive, but I say with confidence that you can have no idea what a vivid, tangible thing is perfect silence. On the surface of the earth there is always some sound or motion, and though it may in itself be imperceptible, yet it deadens the sharp edge of absolute silence. But here there was none. We were buried in the bowels of a huge snow-clad peak. Thousands of feet above us the fresh air rushed over the white snow, but no sound of it reached us. We were separated by a long tunnel and five feet of rock even from the awful chamber of the Dead; and the dead make no noise. The crashing of all the artillery of earth and heaven could not have come to our ears in our living tomb. We were cut off from every echo of the world—we were as men already dead.

And then the irony of the situation forced itself upon me.

71

There around us lay treasures enough to pay off a moderate national debt, or to build a fleet of ironclads, yet we would have bartered them all gladly for the faintest chance of escape. Soon, doubtless, we should be rejoiced to exchange them for a bit of food or a cup of water, and, after that, even for the privilege of a speedy close to our sufferings. Truly wealth, which men spend their lives in acquiring, is a valueless thing at the last.

And so the night wore on.

"Good," said Sir Henry's voice at last, and it sounded awful in the intense stillness, "how many matches have you in the box?"

"Eight, Curtis."

"Strike one and let us see the time."

He did so, and in contrast to the dense darkness the flame nearly blinded us. It was five o'clock by my watch. The beautiful dawn was now blushing on the snow-wreaths far over our heads, and the breeze would be stirring the night mists in the hollows.

"We had better eat something and keep up our strength," I suggested.

"What is the good of eating?" answered Good; "the sooner we die and get it over the better."

"While there is life, there is hope," said Sir Henry.

Accordingly we ate and sipped some water, and another period of time passed. Then Sir Henry suggested that it might be well to get as near the door as possible and halloa, on the faint chance of somebody catching a sound outside. Accordingly, Good, who, from long practice at sea, has a fine piercing note, groped his way down the passage and began. I must say that he made a most diabolical noise. I never heard such yells; but it might have been a mosquito buzzing for all the effect they produced.

After a while he gave it up and came back very thirsty, and had to drink some water. Then we stopped yelling, as it encroached on the supply of water.

So we sat down once more against the chests of useless diamonds in that dreadful inaction, which was one of the hardest circumstances of our fate; and I am bound to say that, for my

72

part, I gave way in despair. Laying my head against Sir Henry's broad shoulder I burst into tears; and I think that I heard Good gulping away on the other side. and swearing hoarsely at himself for doing so.

Ah, how good and brave that great man was! Had we been two frightened children, and he our nurse, he could not have treated us more tenderly. Forgetting his own share of miseries, he did all he could to soothe our broken nerves, telling stories of men who had been in somewhat similar circumstances and miraculously escaped; and, when these failed to cheer us, pointing out how, after all, it was only anticipating an end which must come to us all, that it would soon be over, and that death from exhaustion was a merciful one (which is not true). Then, in a diffident sort of way, as once before I had heard him do, he suggested that we should throw ourselves on the mercy of a higher power, which for my part I did with great vigour.

His is a beautiful character, very quiet, but very strong.

And so somehow the day went as the night had gone, if indeed, one can use these terms where all was densest night, and when I lit a match to see the time it was seven o'clock.

Once more we ate and drank, and as we did so an idea occurred to me.

"How is it," said I, "that the air in this place keeps fresh? It is thick and heavy, but it is perfectly fresh."

"Great heavens!" said Good, starting up, "I never thought of that. It can't come through the stone door, for it's air-tight, if ever a door was. It must come from somewhere. If there were no current of air in the place we should have been stifled when we first came in. Let us have a look."

It was wonderful what a change this mere spark of hope wrought in us. In a moment we were all three groping about on our hands and knees, feeling for the slightest indication of a draught. Presently my ardour received a check. I put my hand on something cold. It was poor Foulata's dead face.

For an hour or more we went on feeling about, till at last Sir Henry and I gave it up in despair, having been considerably hurt by constantly knocking our heads against tusks, chests, and the sides of the chamber. But Good still persevered, saying, with an approach to cheerfulness, that it was better than doing nothing.

"I say, you fellows," he said presently, in a constrained sort of voice, "come here."

Needless to say we scrambled towards him quickly enough.

"Quatermain, put your hand here where mine is. Now, do you feel anything?"

"I *think* I feel air coming up."

"Now listen." He rose and stamped upon the place, and a flame of hope shot up in our hearts. *It rang hollow!*

With trembling hands I lit a match. I had only three left, and we saw that we were in the angle of the far corner of the chamber, a fact that accounted for our not having noticed the hollow sound of the place during our former exhaustive examination. As the match burnt we scrutinized the spot. There was a join in the solid rock floor, and, great heavens! There, let in level with the rock, was a stone ring. We said no word, we were too excited, and our hearts beat too wildly with hope to allow us to speak. Good had a knife, at the back of which was one of those hooks that are made to extract stones from horses' hoofs. He opened it and scratched round the ring with it. Finally he worked it under, and levered away gently for fear of breaking the hook. The ring began to move. Being of stone it had not got set fast in all the centuries it had lain there, as would have been the case had it been of iron. Presently it was upright. Then he thrust his hands into it and tugged with all his force, but nothing budged.

"Let me try," I said impatiently, for the situation of the stone, right in the angle of the corner, was such that it was impossible for two to pull at once. I took hold and strained away, but no results.

Then Sir Henry tried and failed.

Taking the hook again, Good scratched all round the crack where we felt the air coming up.

"Now Curtis," he said, "tackle on, and put your back into it; you

74

are as strong as two. Stop!" He took off a stout black silk hand-kerchief, which, true to his habits of neatness, he still wore, and ran it through the ring. "Quatermain, get Curtis round the middle and pull for dear life when I give the word. *Now!*"

Sir Henry put out all his enormous strength, and Good and I did the same, with such power as nature had given us.

"Heave! heave! It's giving," gasped Sir Henry; and I heard the muscles of his great back cracking. Suddenly there was a grating sound, then a rush of air, and we were all on our backs on the floor with a heavy flag-stone upon the top of us. Sir Henry's strength had done it, and never did muscular power stand a man in better stead.

"Light a match, Quatermain," he said, so soon as we had picked ourselves up and got our breath; "carefully, now."

I did so, and there before us, Heaven be praised, was the *first step of a stone stair.*

"Now what is to be done?" asked Good.

"Follow the stair, of course, and trust to Providence."

"Stop!" said Sir Henry. "Quatermain, get the bit of biltong and the water that are left; we may want them."

I went, creeping back to our place by the chests for that pur-pose, and as I was coming away an idea struck me. We had not thought of the diamonds for the last twenty-four hours or so; in-deed, the very idea of diamonds was nauseous, seeing what they entailed upon us; but, reflected I, I may as well pocket a few in case we ever should get out of this ghastly hole. So I just put my fist into the first chest and filled all the available pockets of my old shooting coat, topping up—this was a happy thought—with a couple of handfuls of big stones out of the third chest.

"I say, you fellows," I sang out, "won't you take some diamonds with you? I've filled my pockets."

"Oh! hang the diamonds!" said Sir Henry. "I hope that I may never see another."

As for Good, he made no answer. He was, I think, taking his last farewell of all that was left of the poor girl who had loved him so well. And curious as it may seem to you, my reader, sitting

75

at home at ease, and reflecting on the vast, indeed the immeasurable, wealth which we were thus abandoning, I can assure you that if you had passed some twenty-eight hours with next to nothing to eat and drink in that place, you would not have cared to cumber yourself with diamonds whilst plunging down into the unknown bowels of the earth, in the wild hope of escape from an agonizing death. If from the habits of a lifetime, it had become a sort of second nature with me never to leave anything worth having behind if there was the slightest chance of my being able to carry it away, I am sure that I should not have bothered to fill my pockets.

"Come on, Quatermain," said Sir Henry, who was already standing on the first step of the stone stair. "Steady, I will go first."

"Mind where you put your feet, there may be some awful hole underneath," I answered.

"Much more likely to be another room," said Sir Henry, while he descended slowly, counting the steps as he went.

When he got to "fifteen", he stopped. "Here's the bottom," he said. "Thank goodness! I think it's a passage. Come on down."

Good went next, and I followed last, and on reaching the bottom lit one of the two remaining matches. By its light we could just see that we were standing in a narrow tunnel, which ran right and left at right angles to the staircase we had descended. Before we could make out any more, the match burnt my fingers and went out. Then arose the delicate question of which way to go. Of course, it was impossible to know what the tunnel was, or where it ran to, and yet to turn one way might lead us to safety, and the other to destruction. We were utterly perplexed, till suddenly it struck Good that when I had lit the match the draught of the passage blew the flame to the left.

"Let us go against the draught," he said; "air draws inwards, not outwards."

We took this suggestion, and feeling along the wall with the hand, whilst trying the ground before us at every step, we departed from that accursed treasure chamber on our terrible quest of life. If ever it should be entered again by living man, which I do not think probable, he will find tokens of our visit in the open chests of jewels, the empty lamp, and the white bones of poor Foulata.

When we had groped our way for about a quarter of an hour along the passage, suddenly it took a sharp turn, or else was bisected by another, which we followed, only in course of time to be led into a third. And so it went on for some hours. We seemed to be in a stone labyrinth which led nowhere. What all these passages are, of course I cannot say, but we thought that they must be the ancient workings of a mine, of which the various shafts and adits travelled hither and thither as the ore led them. This is the only way in which we could account for such a multitude of galleries.

At length we halted, thoroughly worn out with fatigue and with that hope deferred which maketh the heart sick, and ate up our poor remaining piece of biltong and drank our last sup of water, for our throats were like lime-kilns. It seemed to us that we had escaped death in the darkness of the chamber only to meet him in the darkness of the tunnels. As we stood, once more utterly depressed, I thought that I caught a sound, to which I called the attention of the others. It was very faint and very far off, but it *was* a sound, a faint, murmuring sound, for the others heard it too, and no words can describe the blessedness of it after all those hours of utter, awful stillness.

"By heaven! it's running water," said Good. "Come on."

Off we started again in the direction from which the faint murmur seemed to come, groping our way as before along the rocky walls. As we went it became more and more audible, till at last it seemed quite loud in the quiet. On, yet on; now we could distinctly make out the unmistakable swirl of rushing water. And yet how could there be running water in the bowels of the earth? Now we were quite near to it, and Good, who was leading, swore that he could smell it.

"Go gently, Good," said Sir Henry, "we must be close." *Splash!* and a cry from Good.

He had fallen in.

"Good! Good! where are you?" we shouted, in terrified distress. To our intense relief an answer came back in a choky voice.

"All right; I've got hold of a rock. Strike a light to show me where you are."

Hastily I lit the last remaining match. Its faint gleam discovered to us a dark mass of water running at our feet. How wide it was we could not see, but there, some way out, was the dark form of our companion hanging on to a projecting rock.

"Stand clear to catch me," sung out Good. "I must swim for it."

Then we heard a splash, and a great struggle. Another minute and he had grabbed at and caught Sir Henry's outstretched hand, and we had pulled him up high and dry into the tunnel.

"My word!" he said, between his gasps, "that was touch and go. If I hadn't caught that rock, and known how to swim, I should have been done. It runs like a mill-race and I could feel no bottom."

We dared not follow the banks of the subterranean river for fear lest we should fall into it again in the darkness. So after Good had rested a while, and we had drunk our fill of the water, which was sweet and fresh, and washed our faces, that needed it sadly, as well as we could, we started from the banks of this African Styx, and began to retrace our steps along the tunnel, Good dripping unpleasantly in front of us. At length we came to another gallery leading to our right.

"We may as well take it," said Sir Henry wearily; "all roads are alike here; we can only go on till we drop."

Slowly, for a long, long while, we stumbled, utterly exhausted, along this new tunnel, Sir Henry now leading the way.

Suddenly he stopped, and we bumped up against him.

"Look!" he whispered, "is my brain going, or is that light?"

We stared with all our eyes, and there, yes, there, far ahead of us, was a faint, glimmering spot, no larger than a cottage window-pane. It was so faint that I doubt if any eyes, except those which, like ours, had for days seen nothing but blackness, could have perceived it at all.

With a gasp of hope we pushed on. In five minutes there was no longer any doubt: it *was* a patch of faint light. A minute more and a breath of real live air was fanning us. On we struggled. All at once the tunnel narrowed. Sir Henry went on his knees. Smaller yet it grew, till it was only the size of a large fox's earth—it *was* earth now, mind you; the rock had ceased.

A squeeze, a struggle, and Sir Henry was out, and so was Good, and so was I, and there above us the blessed stars, and in our nostrils was the sweet air. Then suddenly something gave, and we were all rolling over and over through grass and bushes and soft wet soil.

I caught at something and stopped. Sitting up I halloed lustily. An answering shout came from just below, where Sir Henry's wild career had been stopped by some level ground. I scrambled to him, and found him unhurt, though breathless. Then we looked for Good. A little way off we discovered him also, jammed in a forked root. He was a good deal knocked about, but soon came to himself.

We sat down together, there on the grass, and the revulsion of feeling was so great that really I think we cried for joy. We had escaped from that awful dungeon, which was so near to becoming our grave. Surely some merciful Power guided our footsteps to the jackal hole, for that is what it must have been, at the termination of the tunnel. And see, yonder on the mountains the dawn we had never thought to look upon again was blushing rosy red.

Presently the grey light stole down the slopes, and we saw that we were at the bottom, or rather, nearly at the bottom, of the vast pit in front of the entrance to the cave. Now we could make out the dim forms of the three Colossi who sat upon its verge. Doubtless those awful passages, along which we had wandered the livelong night, had been originally in some way connected with the great diamond mine. As for the subterranean river in the bowels of the mountain, Heaven only knows what it is, or whence it flows, or whither it goes. I, for one, have no anxiety to trace its course.

Lighter it grew, and lighter yet. We could see each other now, and such a spectacle as we presented I have never set eyes on before or since. Gaunt-cheeked, hollow-eyed wretches, smeared all over with dust and mud, bruised, bleeding, the long fear of imminent death yet written on our countenances, we were, indeed, a sight to frighten the daylight. And yet it is a solemn fact that Good's eye-glass was still fixed in Good's eye. I doubt whether he had ever taken it out at all. Neither the darkness, nor the plunge in the subterranean river, nor the roll down the slope, had been able to separate Good and his eye-glass.

Presently we rose, fearing that our limbs would stiffen if we stopped there longer, and commenced with slow and painful steps to struggle up the sloping sides of the great pit. For an hour or more we toiled steadfastly up the blue clay, dragging ourselves on by the help of the roots and grasses with which it was clothed.

At last it was done, and we stood by the great road, on the side of the pit opposite to the Colossi.

At the side of the road, a hundred yards off, a fire was burning in front of some huts and round the fire were figures. We staggered towards them, supporting one another, and halting every few paces. Presently one of the figures rose, saw us and fell on to the ground, crying out for fear.

"Infadoos, Infadoos! It is we, thy friends."

He rose; he ran to us, staring wildly, and still shaking with fear.

"Oh, my lords, my lords, it is indeed you come back from the dead!—come back from the dead!"

And the old warrior flung himself down before us, and clasping Sir Henry's knees, he wept aloud for joy.

I Came Alive out of Death Valley

by JAMES MILLIGAN

The writer of this story is a man who, in his own words, "didn't stay honest". He saw his father lynched as a child, and he grew up hard, bitter and reckless. The adventure he recounts here befell him just after he had spent some time—very unwillingly—as cook on a cattle ranch. He had betrayed the movements of the herds of cattle to a cattle thief, then being found out, had narrowly escaped. So Milligan judged it better to put as much distance as possible between himself and that cattle ranch.

While I rode I had only one thought in my mind—that the district I was in lay within a few miles of two borders: the State border dividing Old Mexico from the United States.

Four or five hours after nightfall I saw lights ahead, and presently I rode into a small town. At first I thought I'd left the United States and that I was in Mexico, but when I asked a passer-by where I was, he told me the town was Las Cruces, and then I knew it was New Mexico I had struck.

I rode right through the town and on for another hour. I still felt too darned near Texas for comfort. Before dawn I lay down on the open range, and slept for an hour or two.

When I got up I was sore with riding, but I mounted again and rode on.

I rode the pony every day for a fortnight, and then I sold it and went on on foot. My destination was California.

One day, not long after crossing the Californian border out of Nevada, I hit a tiny place called Mojave. A God-forsaken miserable village it was, but it had a saloon, and it was the first inhabited place I'd struck for a long time, because I'd been trailing through the Mojave Desert, so I was mighty glad to find it.

I went to the saloon for a start and drank three beers, one after another, to wash my throat clear of sand. I had just finished my third and was calling for my fourth, when a big tough-looking guy in a white sombrero came and slapped his palm on the bar just beside me and said:

"This one's on me, stranger."

I glanced at him in surprise.

"It suits me," I said. "Have it your own way."

He called for a drink for himself, and we drank together.

"I've been watchin' you," he said. "Sizin' you up, you might say."

"Well? Reached any verdict yet?"

He rolled and lit a cigarette.

"Yeah ... My verdict is that you ain't travellin' for pleasure ..." He glanced down at my shabby clothes. "... nor yet for the good of your health."

"You're dead right. But where is all this health-talk bringin' us?"

The man ignored the question.

"Ever swung a pick?"

"Too often," I answered quite truthfully, remembering Klondyke days.

"Ever worked with mules?"

"Sure," I said—not so truthfully this time.

The man in the white sombrero shot out the third of his rapid-fire questions:

"Like a job?"

"How much?" I could be terse too.

82

"Forty a week."

"That's good pay. What's the job—crowning old ladies with a pick?"

"Worse. Lookin' for gold in Death Valley..."

I knew that name. I'd heard old prospectors in Alaska talking about Death Valley. They had all agreed there was gold there, but that it was so dangerous to enter the place that it wasn't worth all the gold in the world to risk one's neck in it.

The Valley, although quite small, was particularly easy to get lost in. It was subject to a certain kind of wind peculiarly its own which stirred up the sand and changed the whole aspect of the landscape after an hour or two, blotting out old landmarks and erecting new ones, burying new bones and uncovering old ones—bones of men who had lost their lives seeking gold in the place. And at the same time as it obliterated the landmarks whereby men hoped to find their way in and out of the place, it obliterated the landmarks that led to places where gold had been struck, so that a man might strike an El Dorado on one trip into the Valley and never be able to find his way back to it.

Such was the place this stranger was inviting me to try as a rest-cure, and frankly I wasn't particularly attracted to the notion.

"Death Valley, eh? That's somewhere close to these parts, ain't it?"

"No more than a mile or two from where you're standin' right now," said the other man. "If you goes a little way up the road, you'll see the gap in the hills that leads into the Valley. This place is the nearest folks live to the Valley. And listen, buddy, the gold's there. I seen it myself. Why, I could walk to it with my eyes shut."

I'd heard talk not unlike that before.

"If that's so, why give somebody else a rake-off out of the takings when you could keep the whole works for yourself? And, anyway, why pick on me to be the lucky guy?"

"I'll tell you about that. You gotta understand that the climate in Death Valley's so bad that the only safe thing to do is to go in

"Pete had the mules and all the prospecting kit ready for the trip."

for spells of a couple of weeks only, then come out again—besides, don't forget we gotta carry all the water we're gonna need for ourselves an' the mules. Well, don't you see it's gonna pay me better to pay another guy to come with me so I can bring out double the quantity of gold at the end of the two weeks?"

"I sure do—but I still don't see why you need to pick on me."

"Because you blew into this joint at the right time, an' because you look like a guy who could use some dough, that's why. I been waitin' round this burg for over a week for an old partner who was comin' in with me. But he ain't arrived, and I ain't waitin' no longer for him. Well—coming with me?"

"I'll come," I said.

The man with the white sombrero, whose name was Pete (I never knew him as anything else but that), had the mules and all the prospecting kit ready for the trip; and we started off next day.

When we came into the Valley, I didn't think it so bad. It wasn't any hotter than the other parts of the Mojave Desert I'd struck already, and in fact looked very much the same as the other parts—low dunes, heat, and sand-swirls; and that was all there was to it.

Pete acted like a man who knew his way about. When we entered the valley, we headed straight in a certain direction, and didn't swerve from it. We went ahead steadily for a whole day; then Pete yanked his blanket off the mule he was leading and flung it on the sand.

"Here's the place. We camp here," he said.

How he knew the spot, I couldn't figure out at all. All around us there was nothing to be seen but sand, and there were no landmarks of any sort. However, I reckoned that he knew what he was doing. I was being paid a flat rate, and it didn't matter to me whether he struck gold or not.

Next day we started digging, and I began to wonder why we'd brought picks along with us at all, for it was nothing but shovel-work on the soft sand. For three days we dug, and were getting pretty deep, and then a wind sprang up. Within a few seconds of

85

"*For a week we dug, until we'd a hole twice the size of the first one.*"

it starting, we were right in the middle of a hundred-per-cent sandstorm, and, after an hour or so of it, the big hole it had taken us so much labour to dig was completely filled in again.

During the storm, we had just lain doggo inside our tent, with the mules well tethered—there was nothing else we *could* do, and I felt like howling when we came out to find nothing but unbroken sand where our hole had been. Pete didn't worry, though.

"It don't signify," he said cheerfully. "That's just Death Valley all over. Never mind. We'll just have to start in diggin' all over again, that's all."

And we did. For a week we dug, until we'd a hole twice the size of the first one. There was no sign of gold yet, but Pete was sure we'd come to it soon enough. As a matter of fact, I was beginning to get a bit worried about the way Pete kept so darned cheerful, whatever happened; also about the queer way he was going about his prospecting . . .

By that time, too, I was beginning to have worries of a different kind. For one thing, there was the heat. Sometimes it rose as high as 130 degrees, and was hardly ever below 100. Then my body broke out in large patches with warts—or nut-boils—large brown gatherings which itched horribly and kept bursting with a brown discharge that appeared to set up other boils wherever it touched the skin. Pete told me these abominations were the result of drinking the stale water we had been obliged to bring from beyond the Valley.

These weren't the worst pests either. My ill-used carcass became a hunting-ground for the 'greenbank-lice' that flourish locally. These are repulsive creatures much bigger than the common louse, and twice as voracious. They seem to possess the same sort of ability for changing their colour as the chameleon does. Against a black surface they became black, and on the skin they adopted a light green colour—hence the name. When we came out, I had thought that a fortnight wasn't too long to stay at a spell in Death Valley—now I began to wonder . . .

On the eleventh day, the second sandstorm came. And when it did, it just about finished me.

87

One of the mules had strayed, and I chased him. I was just about fifty yards from the mule and a couple of hundred from the camp, when the wind started in to work.

The mule was off like a shot, galloping away into the veils of the flying sand. I let the brute go, and started back to the camp. The sand was blowing up thicker and thicker, and I was scared.

I hadn't gone ten yards before I was more scared still—I couldn't see the camp ... Nothing but a thick blanket of drifting sand, with myself in the middle of it, shut off and caught as securely as a fly in amber.

I tried to cheer myself up by saying I knew quite well in which direction the camp lay, and that I couldn't miss it ... Roughly two hundred yards—I'd take just two hundred paces, and that ought to land me there—it wouldn't do to go past; that would be fatal ...

I started walking, counting my paces carefully. One-ninety-eight, one-ninety-nine, two hundred ... and still there was nothing about me but the sand ...

Maybe it was more than a couple of hundred yards: I'd go on another ten paces. I did—nothing!

Another ten paces—and I was getting real frightened by now. Still nothing but sand—sand under my feet—sand filling the air—sand in my eyes and mouth ...

I lost my head. I ran round in circles, my head bent, half-blinded, calling out to Pete like a lunatic ...

The sandstorm didn't stop for maybe two hours—but how long it was I've no exact idea. By the time it was over, I was deaf and blind and stunned. I remember looking about me in wonderment to find the air clear of sand. I could see. I could see the hot blue sky and the placid dunes all round me. But that was all. Of the camp there was no sign ...

I was lost and I knew it. A new fear gripped: already I was feeling my tongue dry and hard with thirst ...

I began to walk. I walked till sundown, and all through the night. In the morning there was still nothing to be seen about me but the endless hillocks of sand. I went on walking, in an agony of thirst by now, and, when noon came, I could walk no farther.

Twice I dropped in my tracks, and the second time I couldn't get up again.

The next thing I remember is a tiny drop of water—sweeter and fresher than any nectar—on my parched tongue. Then another drop. It was like coming unexpectedly into the Kingdom of Heaven.

I opened my eyes and saw a brown-bearded face looking down at me. I shouted and laughed at the man, calling him Pete—but it wasn't Pete.

"Take it easy, pal," said the stranger. "You'll be outa this sand-pit in a coupla shakes."

I closed my eyes again, Maybe I fainted again, maybe I slept. At any rate when I woke again I was lying in a bed. What a bed! It was so soft and clean that I just had to go off to sleep again.

I was in the saloon back in the village of Mojave. Some old prospector beating it out of Death Valley had found me and brought me along. I was darned lucky, they told me, to get out alive—and so was the old guy who'd brought me out.

Who the old fellow was I never found out; for I never saw him. He just dumped me in the keeping of the saloon boss, then beat it out of town, saying he didn't want to waste time in getting as far away from Death Valley as he could. I was sorry. I'm not a fellow who's too grateful for services rendered, but I'd like to have thanked that guy . . .

They were good to me in that saloon, especially when I told them I was willing to work in the bar for my board. And they knew how to attend to me, for I wasn't the only one by a long chalk that had been carried out of Death Valley into that joint; and I was out of bed in a couple of days.

The first thing I thought about was Pete. I told the saloon-keeper that I'd left my partner in the Valley, and suggested sending a searchparty for him.

"Pete?" said the saloon boss. "Was he a big guy with a white sombrero and a cataract in one eye?"

"That's him."

The boss whistled.

"Say, buddy, I wonder if you knew the company you was travelling in? That guy Pete is nutty as a fruit-cake. He went into the Valley once years ago an' came out ravin' mad. He's been mad ever since, an' keeps goin' back, swearin' he knows where there's a heap of gold. Maybe his madness helps him, for he's the only guy I know who ever comes out again regular."

"God!" I exclaimed. "A looney! You don't mean he's dangerous?"

"Not as a rule. But he gets plumb murderous if anybody says he don't know where his pocket of gold is. If you'd said anything like that, he mighta killed you!"

"So *that's* what was wrong with Pete. I thought he was queer . . . D'you think he'll come out again this time?"

"I guess so."

He did. The very next day, Pete wandered into the bar as casually as though he just stepped in from across the road. I was serving behind the bar, but he didn't give me a second glance.

"Weather's gettin' mighty warm," he remarked as I set up his drink.

I said nothing about the wages he owed me. Somehow, I thought it better not to.

Captured by Chinese Pirates

by PAUL CAREY

When I arrived in Hong Kong, I was informed by the Chinese clerk in the small passenger-freight office that the only available transportation to Singapore, in the next four days, was the small, four-thousand-ton steamer, *Ningpo*. Time was an important factor in my plans, so I booked passage, little knowing that my impatience was to catapult me into more excitement than I had expected to experience in a lifetime.

I found the *Ningpo* moored to a cargo-littered, ramshackle wharf. Built many years before for the China coast and Malaya-East Indies passenger-freight service, she had been defeated by the stern competition from faster and larger ships. From bow to stern, from the low waterline to the tip of her single battered funnel, the *Ningpo* was a ragged old sea-hag.

My first sight of her gave me a curious reaction. I had read in that day's newspapers of the arrest of three Chinese accused of taking part in the pirating of the four-thousand-five-hundred-and-twenty-two-ton Dutch steamer *Van Heutsz*, between Bias Bay and Honghai Bay, just north of Hong Kong.

Half-a-million dollars in money and jewels had been seized, and six wealthy Chinese passengers kidnapped, for eventual ransom payments of ten thousand dollars each. It seemed incredible that this ship, protected by anti-pirate spiked grilles,

"The only available transportation to Singapore was
the small, four-thousand-ton steamer, NINGPO."

steel wire mesh and barred doors could be taken by only twenty Bias Bay pirates, who had booked passage on the *Van Heutsz* disguised as steerage travellers.

Well, I thought, no Bias Bay pirates would molest such a wretched old craft as the *Ningpo*.

I stowed away my baggage in my small cabin and then went topside to present my letter of introduction to the skipper of the *Ningpo*, Captain Digby MacPherson. I found him leaning over the right-wing rail of the bridge. His stocky body was garbed in a wrinkled, soiled uniform of white duck, which seemed on the verge of bursting at every seam under the strain of his massive shoulders, arms and legs. He stood with his feet braced apart, as if set for the constant roll of the ship.

He seemed lost in thought as he watched the esplanade of Hong Kong and its skyline, and said: "This China coast is a rummy place now."

I knew what he meant in general: political unrest, starving refugees, smugglers, cut-throats, pirates and spies.

That was why I was a little surprised by the lack of anti-pirate security measures aboard the *Ningpo*. No special guards were aboard the ship; absent, also, were the heavy steel mesh wire and the boxing-in of stairways to the bridge which separated the forepart of the steamer, where the steerage passengers were carried, from the officers' and first-class passengers' cabins. Pirates always travelled aboard passenger boats disguised as poor Chinese, to avoid attracting attention, as they would if they travelled cabin-class.

I politely inquired of Captain MacPherson the reason for the omission.

"I've been sailing this coast for a quarter of a century," he snorted, "and only twice have I been attacked. The first time was when I was a few hours out of Hong Kong on the *Taiyuan*, and my second mate spotted two junks trailing us. We dropped anchor between Macao and the island of Ma Las Chao, and battened down the hatches on the steerage passengers. The junks came closer, and suddenly started firing at the bridge with muzzle-loading cannon. By this time, they were within throwing distance, so my officers and I heaved fused dynamite sticks at the fat targets in the water. Both junks were blown out of the water; then we went through the steerage quarters and found ten pirates hiding there. Of course, they lost their heads in prison—the penalty in China at the time for almost every crime.

"The second time was on the *Ningpo*, and south of Swatow. At Amoy, some pirates had come aboard, as steerage passengers. Shortly after midnight they came crawling like lizards up over the bridge, yelling and shooting off their pistols. As quick as they showed their heads, my officers and I picked them off with submachine guns."

He nodded grimly. "Word gets around fast, up and down the China coast, so I suppose the pirates figure that we're just too dangerous to monkey with."

According to Captain MacPherson, piracy has menaced the China coast for years. The year 1938 saw the rise of a hanger-on of the gambling and opium dens of Macao, Wong Kung, who organised a pirate fleet of fast motor junks and sleek launches.

For eight years he terrorised active shipping around Hong Kong and Canton, using the island of Ma La Chao as his stronghold; most of the large passenger-steamer "jobs" were handled by him. Wong was captured in January of 1946 by Chinese Communists, who turned him over to the Portuguese authorities in Macao. Wong was shot through the head and back while trying to escape.

Madame Wong had taken over the fleet of fast motor boats and sloops, and it is rumoured that she also knows the location of the fifty million dollars Wong stole and cached. Latest reports say that she is still preying upon coastal shipping in the South China Seas, and is seen frequently in the nightclubs of Macao, gambling and dancing, daring the authorities to arrest her. Sometimes she disappears and, simultaneously, reports of ship and junk pirates appear in the headlines of the Hong Kong newspapers.

Chief Officer Duncan, a gaunt man with an equine face, came

up the bridge ladder and we were introduced. He had more to add to Captain MacPherson's pirate lore of the China Seas.

"The really big jobs are pulled by big-time operators like Madame Wong. A gang of pirates board the passenger vessels only when a carefully worked out plan has been made absolutely foolproof. Sometimes they have bribed members of the crew to give them information on the layout of the ship, the officers and the changing of the watches. A few spies will make as many as three and four trips on a steamer to 'case' the job. Success in grabbing such a big prize as a five-thousand-ton steamer depends on smooth team work. Lately, they've been knocking over the big ships, one after the other."

An hour later, the *Ningpo* dropped her mooring lines and headed for the open sea.

I walked forward after dinner, and glanced down the well-deck. Pinpoints of lighted cigarettes glowed in the darkness and, as my eyes became accustomed to the night, I could see men, women and children sprawled about the deck with their possessions, filling every inch of space, many sleeping on their piled-up, mat-wrapped bundles. A fearful stench of tobacco, opium smoke, foul clothing, chickens, pig offal and strange herb-like food, made the air reek.

As I stared down at these unfortunate victims of China's disorder, I wondered if there were any pirates among them.

I went below to my cabin, undressed and climbed into the bunk. I don't know how long I had been asleep, but suddenly I was jarred into wakefulness by the rapid hammering of a sub-machine gun and the sharp explosions of pistol fire.

The motion of the *Ningpo* had slackened, and the strong, constant vibrations of her engines had died away completely.

I sprang to my feet and looked out of the porthole. A murmur of human alarm was sweeping through the ship, and there was the rapid patter of feet on the deck above me, more shooting and hoarse, desperate cries.

I put on my bathrobe and stepped cautiously into the corridor. It was empty, but lights were being snapped on in nearby cabins, and startled inquiries gathered volume. There came the sounds of human bodies being hurled against railings and bulkheads, and then splintering crashes, as if camphor-wood chests and crates were being toppled over in the well-deck and in the steerage quarters. A long, sustained wail of fright spiralled from this section, rising to a blood-chilling Chinese shrieking that could be heard in every part of the ship.

I ran up to the boat-deck, just below the bridge. The well-deck under the dazzling beams of floodlights was a seething sea of alarmed Chinese. A smothering tide of humanity was swarming up the forward ladders, shoving, screaming, beating with bare hands on the barred door. Sub-machine guns spat viciously from the hurricane-deck above the bridge, and the surging steerage passengers fell back, toppling head over feet down the iron rungs to a squirming heap at the bottom. The ship's officers had fired over their heads.

I saw dark forms crawling up over the front of the ship toward the bridge from the well-deck, with the aid of every conceivable sort of crevice their experienced toes could grip. Now and then one of them fell off and thudded to the steel deck below, jerking spasmodically in agony.

Bullets were whining ominously close, and I threw myself upon the deck, cursing the curiosity that had brought me above decks. There was no chance to get below again. The alleyways, ladders and decks amidships were swarming with hysterical white passengers. Bullet after bullet was tearing through the wood about me, showering me with splinters.

Suddenly, a screaming rocket trailing red fire snaked high into the night sky, and then a white one. The whole ship was illuminated starkly, and in the well-deck I saw a number of pirates with rifles herding the deck-passengers below. My heart fell. The pirates must have gained control of the ship!

The machine-gun fire still raged on the hurricane-deck and there were angry retorts from the rifles and pistols of the Chinese marauders. Had Captain MacPherson been killed? What of Chief Officer Duncan? I made a dash down an alleyway. In the

"*Suddenly a screaming rocket trailing red fire snaked high into the sky.*"

darkness I collided with someone and then I felt the cold contact of a revolver muzzle against my bare stomach.

"You go to dining-room, please!" a fierce Chinese voice barked in my face.

I turned and walked ahead of him, more frightened than ever I had been in my life. Most of the first-class passengers were already in the saloon; a white-haired missionary and his wife were down on their knees praying; around them were grouped a big-game hunter bound for Sumatra, a planter returning to Malaya, a woman journalist from London, a young doctor for the government hospital in Macassar, two white Russian women, and a corpulent Dutch planter's wife and her buck-toothed daughter.

We all sat white-faced and trembling about the tables. Four Chinese pirates, incongruously dressed in European attire, stood against each wall, their sub-machine guns pointed at us. They looked efficient and dangerous. I wondered where the captain was.

A few minutes later, Chief Officer Duncan was pushed roughly into the room. He was bleeding from the mouth and forehead, and he staggered badly, as if stunned by his violent capture and subsequent beating. He fell weakly into a chair beside me, breathing heavily, his chin resting on his heaving chest. I whispered a question to him about the captain, but he didn't seem to hear me.

Later, I learned that Duncan had sprung out of his cabin at the first sounds of the pirates' attack and dashed into the wheelhouse. There, a Chinese pirate was bent over the binnacle as he whirled the spokes. His plan obviously was to set the *Ningpo* on a course that would bring her closer to shore in the vicinity of Bias Bay.

The Chief Officer lunged, and the pirate heard him, turned and fired at almost point-blank range, but the bullet whined over Duncan's head and shattered a window of the wheelhouse. The crashing impact of his fist knocked the pirate back across the wheelhouse, shrieking for help. He tried to leap to his feet, but the Chief Officer brought the pirate's pistol down hard on the un-

98

protected, bobbing head. Duncan swung the engine-room telegraph handle to "Stand by" and then whistled down the tube, shouting his presence to the chief engineer and explaining the situation topside.

"I'm barricaded in here," Stevens cried up the speaking-tube. "They'll have to blast me or my gang out."

Chief Officer Duncan was putting the ship back on course when two pirates burst in upon him and, before he could fire, they floored him with a rifle-butt blow in the mouth, breaking three teeth and splitting his lips. The other pirate pistol-whipped him on the head until he fell to his knees.

Presently, the door to the dining-room opened again and there entered a small, wiry Chinese in khaki shirt and pants, with a shoulder-holster strapped under his arm. He motioned us to our feet with the huge .45. Methodically, the white passengers were stripped of valuables, which were lumped into a small canvas bag carried by the pirate.

The shooting outside had ceased, and we realised that all resistance, save in the engine-room stronghold, had been overcome by the pirates. As we sat there, ruminating upon our fate, a turn of events was shaping the crew's quarters. They had been hemmed in there by a force of pirates, and, unknown to them, Captain MacPherson, not far away in the paint locker with a sub-machine gun, was waiting until the ship quietened down before putting into effect his strategy of rescue.

Our first indication that a reversal aboard ship was in the making was a sudden burst of fire from an automatic weapon. The pirates guarding us in the dining-room became apprehensive, darting excited glances out of the portholes. Shots crashed into the walls of the saloon, and we fell to the floor. Abruptly the lights went out, and the din of battle exploded again.

It was a heartening sound to us now. We knew that somewhere out on the decks a surprise attack had been made upon the pirates, and they were losing ground.

Captain MacPherson was the hero of the retaking of the ship. Stepping out of the paint locker, he had crept towards the crew's quarters, sized up the situation of the pirates looting the lockers there, while the Malay crew watched sullenly. Slanting the muzzle of the machine-gun over the porthole, he had rained death upon the surprised pirates.

The Malay crew shot out of the doorway, brandishing stools, benches, clubs, knives and lengths of chain. Captain MacPherson organised them quickly, leading them through a manhole in the port-alleyway and down into the quarters amidships. There they swarmed over the pirates' defences, and drove them back into the stern.

Within an hour every pirate alive or not wounded had been tossed into the barred isolation cabins below deck. The leader of the gang was dead, shot through the neck, and twelve of his men had also been killed.

Of the crew and passengers of the *Ningpo*, one was dead—a Chinese steerage passenger struck by a stray ricocheting bullet; about twenty-five Chinese deck-travellers were suffering from superficial wounds.

The *Ningpo* headed back to Hong Kong, where the pirates were led handcuffed to prison—eventually to lose their heads.

Ants

by W. J. BLACKLEDGE

I start without preamble, with an episode that has burned itself into my memory, an incident that nothing but death can efface. I was sweating with fear. Since this is a confession of things experienced during twenty months with the famous Hell's Broth Militia, let me confide the state of my feelings during a typical experience by way of opening.

I did not find it easy to keep my nerve while tied to a stake, and that stake planted firmly on top of an ant-hill, the great red ants swarming up my legs, crawling nearer to the more vulnerable parts of my person.

The yelling natives who danced around me were, of course, offering me the usual bogey-bogey stuff; and while their mad antics did not make a great impression upon me, they hardly helped towards steadiness of nerves. I knew my East. I had had experience enough to realise there was a way out of even this desperate plight. But all my reassuring thoughts could not stop the cold sweat pouring.

These insane devils were intent upon making me squirm. Tying a man to a stake on an ant-hill so that millions of red ants might get busy nipping the sense out of him—well, that was their queer idea of entertainment. Amusement seems to be largely a matter of geography. In the United States it is all-in wrestling, or

"*There was a sickening irritation as the crawling
things began to nip.*"

some other fashion of the moment. In Europe the making or un-making of war. In the less civilised parts of the East, slow torture.

I know of no kind so slow and terrifying as this. It is not new in the East. It is as old and cruel as the Himalayas. For the first hour or so I had been able to stand it with a fair show of nonchalance. There was a sickening irritation as the crawling things began to nip, a shivering and a flesh-creeping in spite of all one's efforts to remain stolid. The irritations increased slowly, insidiously. The crawling hordes were advancing. I found myself thrusting with the surface muscles, tightening and relaxing the flesh, as a horse will against the persistent flies. The muscular actions were involuntary. I could not stop them.

I had been stripped of all clothing. Wherever the myriads of red devils advanced, nipping, stinging, piercing, I shivered and shook in spite of myself. I stared straight ahead, not daring to look down upon limbs fast turning crimson as the massed army of ants surged upwards. Their progress was damnably slow. They would crowd an area of flesh... Others climbed over them... inching their way upwards. I did not mind about my limbs so much. They would heal. I was suddenly concerned about my face, and more especially about my sight...

The more they advanced, the more the natives yelled and danced about me—women as well as men. It seemed that the whole of that tiny village hidden away in the mountains had assembled to watch the performance, to shriek with glee as the sahib was tortured until he cried out for mercy or went utterly berserk.

I had made up my mind about that. They would get no humiliating appeal out of me. The mental torture would not get control if I'd just keep my eyes staring straight ahead and my mind from dwelling on the possibilities of these millions of little butchers. Incredible the thousands of spots on one's person that can be pricked and bitten at one and the same time. Again and again I dragged my thoughts and my mind from these one hundred thousand irritations. Hands, arms, the surfaces long exposed to India's merciless sun, these were not so easily affected. But the soft and tender parts that had always had the protection of clothing ...

And all the while the men and women danced, shrieked with crazy laughter, tried to attract my attention with actions and remarks so obscene that they cannot be repeated. Seated on a raised dais about fifty yards away was Be-akle Lenhai, the Mad Fakir, the demented devil responsible for my horrible predicament. He was rocking, hugging himself with mirth—if mirth there be in such a ferocious and twisted mentality. He it was who had started all this trouble on the North-West Frontier of India.

He was well-named. Be-akle means witless. He was the maddest thing this side of Gehenna. He was waging a holy war. His native magic had brought the most fierce of the Mohammedans to his biddings. His avowed object was to raise by fire and sword the new Moslem Empire. He was no religious mendicant subsisting on alms. He took. Men gathered to his aid as he advanced across the mountainous no-man's-land that lies between Afghanistan and the North-West Frontier. He pronounced terrible curses on all who attempted to thwart him, his favourite being "May you perish by fire!" He had advanced along a trail of burning villages, wrecking, plundering, violating.

He was the wild fanatic who was to descend from High Asia down upon the plains of India and sweep away the white infidels. Once across this no-man's-land and he would head a gigantic wave of turbulent tribes down through the thirty miles of rocky defile that is the Khyber Pass, and so on to India. If he were not checked. And checked he had been, on several occasions—driven back into his mountain fastnesses by the one force he dreaded: Hell's Broth Militia.

I was the first of the leaders of this force to come into his hands. With such a man, such a situation, anything might ensue. I knew that when the little red devils had done their damndest, when I had reached the state of being unable to register anything further for the amusement of Lenhai and his mob, he would start the fire at my ankles. "May you perish by fire!"

I stared at the ragged beard tinged with red henna. How appropriate, I thought. Red ants! Fire! I must keep a tight hold on myself. This would never do. But it was difficult. I should start to laugh and blubber if I let these gnawing itchings get the better of me. Be-akle's eyes were glistening. Sometimes there was a piercing intensity. Other times an obscure observation of the beyond. Or was it my mental state? I can vouch for the fellow's magnetism, at all events. Immense stature. The frame of an ox.

Mad he undoubtedly was. Otherwise he would have been dead long ago. The Moslems the world over, and more so in that wild region, respect the brother whose mind is deranged. To them such an affliction comes straight from the directing hand of Allah himself. Such a man will always command an audience. Such a one is capable of anything.

There was method in his madness. It was the hot season of the year, the time of the year when fighting is the only industry in the wild regions beyond the Pass. Until the autumn came round there would be no further scratching at the soil by these warlike tribes. So the Mad Fakir, with the lust for blood gone to his head, was gathering an ever-increasing army of Waziris, Mahsuds, the Madda Khel, the Zadrians of Khost, and all the rest of the rag-tag and bob-tail of racial tribes.

And all that stood between him and the northern mouth of the Khyber Pass was Hell's Broth Militia. True, he would meet the regular British Indian troops if he reached the Pass; but it was our job to prevent him and all his kind from trekking down to that gateway.

If only I could get one hand free! Just to scratch at these nipping devils! My eyes smarted with the irritations. Tears mingled with the sweat. I was not blubbering. It was as if some strong irritant had reached them so that the tear ducts burst. But damnably humiliating just the same.

And then, as I continued staring straight ahead, desperately trying to keep my mind off the gnawing red ants, a woman walked into my line of vision. She was different. She was without veil. These folk of the hills, it should be understood, are not Indians. Many of them, though sunburnt, are as fair-skinned as

105

the people of the West. But this was no woman of the hills. Nor was she an Indian. What was she doing in this God-forsaken spot?

She had taken her stand by Lenhai's side, staring curiously at me as if I were some new anthropological body brought forth for her inspection. The thoroughbred woman of the hills has remarkable eyes—eyes of a sapphire blue that distinguish her from the pure Indian type. But the eyes of this woman were purple-black, her face a pale oval with darker shades about the eyes and the soft column of throat. Her *burka*, or cloak, had fallen back, revealing the black hair plastered down the sides of her small head, Madonna fashion. For the rest, she was dressed like the hill woman—a three-quarter-length tight-fitting jacket of green velvet, baggy trousers of scarlet silk tight round the ankles, and voluminous cloak.

By the side of the towering Lenhai, she looked slim, slight, small-boned—but there was the devil in her smouldering black eyes. She neither laughed nor yelled but stood at gaze, talking quietly to the Mad Fakir. She was so striking that for several minutes her presence forced itself through my absorption with the biting ants. But I soon realised it was no good looking to her for help. She may not have been one of these crazy hill people. She may not become excited at the spectacle of my ant-ridden body. Except for her eyes, she appeared utterly nonchalant.

Who was this mystery woman? Was she the power behind the throne of Lenhai?

Would it be of any use yelling to her? It was a forlorn hope. But my whole body was creeping and shaking by this time. I was ready to grasp at any frail straw. I guess I was in a pretty desperate state. And there'd be some distraction from my gnawing agony in bawling at this cold, indifferent creature with the smouldering eyes. I yelled at the top of my voice, shrieked so loudly that I was heard above the din and racket of the dancing hill folk. I shouted not in an appeal but in hot anger:

"You are no Moslem woman of the Hills! Does it please you to watch while I am humiliated ... bitten alive?"

I shouted in English. Most of the mob, who knew only their native *pushtu*, did not understand. At all events it had the effect of checking the wild orgy. They stopped and stared towards the woman whom I had addressed in the tongue of the *ferungi*—the language of the people beyond the Pass and over the seas.

As for the woman, she stared coldly, the suggestion of a smile curving her thin lips. There was a weird silence for several seconds. The people continued to stare at her, expectantly. It was as if they looked to her for guidance. In that sudden cessation of noise the gnawing of the thousands of red ants was intensified a thousand and a thousand times. Involuntarily I squirmed. Sweat dropped from every pore even as the little red devils bit and bored. For now they had reached my neck and I was shaking my head to keep them down—so like an animal with the persistent flies!

My actions raised a laugh, a laugh that spread into an uproar. I suppose I did look funny, screamingly funny, jerking my head about like an infuriated horse!

They were at the corners of my mouth—where the saliva frothed. I, too, was biting. I was biting and spitting and making all manner of facial contortions to rid my face of the creeping insects. I knew that if they got to my eyes I should be reduced to gibbering terror. And that would be one real triumph for these guffawing swine.

But one thing I noticed through all this increasing agony and horror. The mystery woman was talking earnestly to the Mad Fakir. Was she interceding on my behalf? I prayed as they talked. I prayed as I fought against the creeping red army that now threatened to choke me, blind me. They were filling my nostrils—no matter how hard I exhaled. A sickening terror engulfed me. I spewed violently. I should have gone right out then, I guess, had not someone come along with a heavy broom of twigs and started to sweep the filthy creatures from my body.

That broom was harsh and incredibly rough against my flesh, but it was a heaven-sent relief to me. It was jabbed ruthlessly about my head and neck and shoulders. It was swept over

107

me from head to foot in no gentle manner. But it was effective. The relief, the reaction was so intense that I very nearly fainted.

Then the cords were cut and I was dragged clear of the ant-hill. I began to put on my clothes. Armed Pathans stood by. The woman was watching from a few yards distant. Her face was expressionless—except for the smouldering eyes.

"I couldn't begin to express my thanks ..." I began.

"Don't trouble," said she. "There may be worse to come."

As I was led away I wondered greatly just what she meant. She spoke in English with an accent that had nothing to do with the "Free Land of the Hills", not with India beyond the Pass. That set me puzzling. Where had I heard that peculiar accent before? This was no native of the East. At all events, she had power, the power to set me free from that digustingly filthy torture. She had given me a breathing space.

The ants had left their mark—or marks. It was like a terrific intensification of prickly heat. I itched to claw at a hundred places at once. Nevertheless, I was suddenly filled with hope, optimistic enough to believe that I still had a chance, that I might even make a getaway!

Every village in the hill country is walled and fortified. There are incessant feuds among the clans which make such precautions necessary. At any rate, the feuds were constant until the Mad Fakir came along to unite the clans in holy war against the infidels. But the fortifications remained. One would need to be something of a magician to get clear of these walls, seven feet thick, and which were patrolled night and day by hillmen armed to the teeth.

I lay in my stone cell and pondered these things. The walls of my prison were of solid stone, like most of the buildings in these villages—for the country was just one gigantic mass of rocks and stones. The only opening besides the door was a circular one high up in the wall. It did not look big enough for me to worm my way through. I am fairly heavily built and top all of five feet ten. The only piece of furniture in the room was a *charpoy*, a bed

108

made of a wooden frame with cord laced across after the manner of a spring mattress. I up-ended this by the wall. It put me six feet up the wall, but even then I could only just get my head to the aperture.

The light was still good. I could see across the courtyard of this cluster of buildings. Beyond was the village proper. The natives were back at their daily tasks. A camel caravan had arrived, and there was much bartering and trading in the bazaar. It all looked peaceful and happy enough. Veiled and heavily-cloaked women, with gaily-trousered legs, shuffled through the dust of the high-ways and byways. Stalwart and muscular Pathans, many of them over six feet tall, strode hither and yon. They went about their peaceful occupations heavily armed. It was a habit with the hillmen. They and their forebears had lived that way for centuries—always ready for a fighting feud.

I measured the loophole. It was just possible that I could squeeze through. There were armed men patrolling beneath. At sunset they would bow their heads to the dust in supplication to Allah, for the Moslem faith was very strong in these folk, I decided that when the hour of prayer came I should take a chance. I must not let this night go by without trying. God knows what was awaiting me on the morrow. I was not afraid of death. Indeed I preferred it to the frightful tortures that these fanatics of the hills could inflict.

With the setting of the sun, however, my chances of escape dwindled considerably. For the great door was suddenly thrust open, and the strange woman who had been responsible for my release from the ant-hill entered. She locked the door behind her, then sat down beside me on the *charpoy*. I was too taken aback to speak. We stared at each other for several seconds. The creature's face was as expressionless as that of a Chinese. Only her eyes were alive.

"Digger Craven," she said, "you want to get back to your company of killers, don't you? Even now you are planning ways and means of escape?"

"Where did you get hold of my nickname?"

"Never mind that. Would you like to walk out of this village a free man?"

"That hardly needs answering. Who are you?"

"Mahrila is my name. That is all you may know. In exchange for a little information you will be escorted to within safe distance of your camp. Lenhai has promised that."

"What on earth is there that I can tell you?"

She very soon made herself clear. Apparently there was quite a lot I could tell—the strength of my company of irregulars, the numbers and dispositions of the garrisons along the Khyber Pass, the recent movements of troops on the Frontier, and strength and type of arms, the secret of the ammunition dumps, the strength of the new flying unit, and what exactly was this automatic gun that had recently appeared at the Frontier posts?

All of which was very interesting. Only a magician or the GOC could answer such questions. And so I told her. She was convinced I was feigning ignorance of the military situation. Even if I could not supply all the information she sought—surely there was much that I knew? Just how much? Wasn't it worth imparting in exchange for my life? Or did I prefer a slow, tortuous death? I protested—and wondered where the devil I had heard that accent before. It wasn't French, nor German, nor Italian ...

"What are you doing in the Pathan country, Mahrila?"

"I belong to this country."

"That's just a cheap lie."

She shrugged, repeated her offer.

"You don't belong to this land. You are not a Moslem—or you would be at prayers now."

"What does it matter who I am? I'm offering you release in return for a little information. Are you going to prove yourself as big a fool as you looked on the ant-hill?"

I wriggled. A thousand sores were pricking.

"What do you suppose I got you out of that plight for? Merely because you are a white man? Tcha! I want these few facts. You can give them. Stop playing the fool. Lenhai has less patience than I."

110

"I am not a staff officer. I know nothing of these things."

I tried to be patient, but I could see she did not believe me.

"If you think I am being terribly heroic, you're all wrong. I tell you I don't know."

"But you are an officer of the Kurram Militia. You must know something of these things."

And so it went on, a battle of wits, for the better part of an hour. The wench had a bee in her bonnet, and it was very nearly as big as the beetle in Be-akle Lenhai's turban. I'd known that these folk of the hills were crazy about their religious ideals, but I had never realised just how crazy they could be until I fell into their hands.

"You came here secretly with your native servant. Why?"

"You know why," I snapped, scratching at the infuriating heat spots. "I came to find out just what Lenhai was doing with this clan. The fellow has become a dangerous menace, not merely to the Frontier, but to India as well. He has caused more murder and bloodshed and terror among the tribes . . ."

"You're just a spy!"

"Don't be theatrical. I mistook you for an intelligent woman. I am doing a job of work, as an officer. You know what the Kurram Militia is. We are policing these parts. Lenhai is wrecking the countryside. He's got to be stopped. Now be sensible and show me how I can get out of this fort."

"On condition that you give me what I ask for!"

"For heaven's sake, woman! I haven't any information to give. What are you doing in their galley? Don't you realise that if Lenhai is allowed to carry on he might well start an ugly war?"

"But of course. That is what he intends. And once his plans are complete, all the armies of the British on the Frontier will not stop him."

She did not, I thought, possess those eerie-looking orbs for nothing. Probably she was just as mentally deranged as the Mad Fakir himself. Certainly she looked capable of anything. But what possible interest could she have in this Moslem's holy war? She was not of the Faith. Yet she was accepted by these people.

111

Suddenly she swung round, stared hard with her smouldering eyes.

"If what you say is true, you are of no use to us. Why should I not kill you now?"

"What good would that do? And what d'you suppose I should be doing while you are using that knife of yours? That pretty neck shouldn't be difficult to twist. The advantage would be mine—since you are between me and the door."

"Maybe Lenhai will persuade you to talk tomorrow."

She jumped to her feet and went hurriedly out of the cell, crashing the door behind her. Apparently she had suddenly lost interest in me. Perhaps she had just realised her danger—alone in this cell with a desperate man, whose thousands of irritating sores made it extremely difficult for him to keep a level head. I have no doubt that my ferocious bites were responsible for much of my reckless behaviour from then on. I had missed the opportunity of making a getaway while the guards were at prayer.

And now darkness had descended, but the light from a torch in the courtyard illumined my prison sufficiently for me to set to work. Once more I up-ended the *charpoy* and climbed up to the opening in the wall. I made a cautious survey. There were two guards patrolling beneath, typical of their clan—muscular giants armed to the teeth. The situation looked perfectly hopeless. Maybe if it had not been for the ghastly sores gnawing at me from head to foot I should not have made the attempt. But my condition was such that I would have welcomed death—rather than sit still in that stifling cell with nothing to do but dwell on a lacerated flesh and scratch ...

I moved round gingerly on my perilous perch. The drop would be about ten feet—a mere trifle. Out I went, feet first, lowering myself slowly. I hung by finger-tips for breathless seconds—then dropped. There I lay panting. It was a lovely getaway—so far! I'd hardly made a sound. A dozen yards away the two guards stood chatting. A murmur of sound came from beyond the courtyard wall. I sat crouched in the shadow of what had been my prison

112

"Hot lead spattered around me as I struggled to scale
the wall, tearing my legs on the spikes."

only a few moments ago and thought hard. If I could cross the yard and scale the wall, I'd have more than a sporting chance.

It could be done, providing I crept round the walls and kept out of the beam of light thrown by the torch. I began inching my way through the shadows. I was then as cunning as any hillman! It seemed that I crawled for hours, pausing frequently to make sure I was not discovered. Reaching an angle of the prison wall, I sat and rested for a while. I was then out of sight of the guards. They seemed to be satisfied to patrol within a few yards of the cell door.

I was appreciably nearer the outer wall of the fort, a matter of half a dozen yards. Child's play, thought I, and chuckled softly. Looking back, I now know that mentally I was more than a trifle sub-normal, otherwise I could not have made the grade.

Clearing the intervening space, I crouched under the court-yard wall. It was all of ten feet high and spiked. Still the two guards patrolled up and down, blissfully ignorant of the fact that I was no longer in that cell. I slipped off my belt, threw it over a spike, began to haul myself up. A shot rang out. It whistled close to my ear, flattened itself against the wall. There was a yelling and scampering of feet. Hot lead spattered around me as I struggled to scale the wall, tearing my legs on the spikes. Something pierced my arm like a sizzling hot needle. Stopped one? But I was over and had tumbled to the ground in a heap before my shouting pursuers had reached the wall.

The shoulder burned and ached intolerably, adding to the general soreness and irritation of the ant bites. There was no time to heed such things. The bawling of angry and excited men was too close. The shadows of night, however, were all in my favour. The village, like all habitations of these mountain regions, had no street lighting. A few torches lit up the bazaar quarter. I gave it a wide berth. The tortuous alleys afforded plenty of cover. I slunk along the shadows of the mean little streets.

Soon the whole place was roused. Men and women were racing about in all directions. Their voices proclaimed the fact that the *ferungi* had escaped and was hiding somewhere in the village. I was in a spot. The village wall, seven or eight feet thick, would be crawling with snipers. No man went around these fortified habitations of the mountains unarmed, unless he were very old.

I flattened against the wall of a house as a great giant of a fellow came tearing round the corner. He pulled up sharply. I lifted my foot to his shin. We went down together. A decision of split seconds. I had to keep this hulking brute quiet. That was the essential thing. My elbow was under his chin. I worked like a madman, pounding a vulnerable spot. He beat the dust with his one free arm, tried to wrap his legs around me for the throw. But I had his gun and was using the butt to smash him into silence.

The next moment I felt myself lifted in the air. I came down with a crash, hitting my jaw against the butt of the gun, struggled clumsily for several minutes, trying to regain my breath. Like all hillmen, the fellow possessed amazing strength. He continued to throw me about, even though his face was a bleeding pulp and his jaw broken. I bent back one of his arms, farther and farther, heard the sickening crack.

Still we fought on, scrabbling and rolling in the dust. At all events, he had had no opportunity to shout and thus warn others of my presence. In those inflamed minutes I fought with death in mind, not knowing, not caring whether this were the end. My thumb broke on the leathery texture of his neck. I can see now the foaming mouth, the twisted jowl dripping blood, and the icy glare in his eyes. While I laboured and panted, the sweat poured, salting excruciatingly the ant-bitten sores. I was sick with the intolerable throbbing and gnawing of the bullet wound. But, somehow, I fought on, feeling that only this brute and his incredible strength stood between me and freedom.

These men of the hills are totally different from the Indians, bigger even than the average Arabian. Rarely does one come upon a Pathan less than six feet in height. They are heavy and muscular, with an enormous spread of shoulders. And though they are like the rest of their Eastern brothers in that they know hardly anything about the use of fists, these hillmen are adept in a certain kind of native wrestling.

That I discovered to my cost when I fought with the hillman in the dimness of that grimy alley. Once his champing jaw closed over my jugular vein. But he could not grip. His jaw was broken. He gasped with the pain of the effort. I was sticky with blood—my adversary's as well as my own. We both became pretty well spent, pawing stupidly, clutching less and less firmly. I dared not leave him while he showed any fight at all. God! How beastly it all was! I trembled with rage because I had not the strength to lift the gun again and finish him. I lay on him, the dead weight of my body slumped over him, in exhaustion. Just how long I remained there, why we were never discovered, I cannot say. I was dimly aware that the night was advancing, the cries of the searchers, the scurrying of feet, the hullabaloo of a maddened populace deprived of its prey—grew gradually fainter, died away.

And now I was in greater peril than ever. I realised the urgency of getting to my feet, getting on my way, before the dawn came up. But I could not rise. Hours passed while I lay crumpled over that stinking carcass, precious hours; and I hadn't the wit to stagger to my feet. I could have cried with the bitter impotence of the situation. Must I give in, after all the effort I'd made? Again and again I tried, crawled a few inches, dragging along by the wall, slumping there to regain breath. The Pathan lay still. I stared at the figure. Dead? I never knew. Nor cared.

Up on my feet by the wall, panting like a wounded stone crusher. Mine a livery of ineptitude. Helpless. Hopeless. Then a staggering sort of run—only to pitch headlong into the dust. Whither? I had not the foggiest notion. Did not know whether my direction was towards the village wall. I was doing the craziest sort of jogtrot. Up and down, careering like one drugged with hashish, with one idea fixed firmly in my mind—keep moving ... keep moving. Had I gone forth with all my faculties fully alive I should probably have stumbled into someone. I know that

116

figures slunk past me as I lay in the dust. It seemed that fate was on my side in that last desperate effort.

Breath hiccoughing in sobs. A deadening pain up the wounded arm to neck and shoulder. The incessant prickling of a thousand bites. A thumb missing—or was it just dead with numbness? Things to remember whenever the long, long hours of that ghastly night are recalled.

Other memories, seething and sullen yet vivid, of those darkened streets that wound endlessly, of sudden alarms as I snuggled into the dust, my nose within a few inches of passing feet, gaily slippered feet, familiar silk-trousered legs, heavy sandals of stalwart men, giant Pathans, and their womenfolk drifting back to well-guarded homes, scraps of conversation ... They seemed pretty certain I could not leave the village, that I'd never get beyond the fortified walls, even in the darkness.

Then silence. The village slept. With the strange quietude that precedes the dawn I was recovering sufficiently to gain some sense of direction. And now I had the gun and cartridge belts of that figure I had left slumped in the dirt. My one desire was to get beyond this village and down into the valley where I might find a cave. Then sleep. Heavens! How I longed for sleep!

The wall. Figures patrolling. It would be easy enough to reach the top, for there were jutting steps at intervals used by the guards. But how to get by these armed patrols? There was one squatting on his haunches immediately above, his back towards me, staring out into the blackness. If I brained him with the gun, how long would it be before he was discovered and I was followed? I was in no state to out-distance a fit man. To walk was painful enough.

I had the solution of that difficulty. He must not be discovered. I crept, taking the jutting stones slowly and painfully.

When one's life depends on every little move ... I reached the topmost step, my chin over the rim of the wall. On the right and left flanks dim figures moved restlessly, heard rather than seen. But the squatting figure little more than a yard away never moved. It was too much to hope that he would be asleep. I squatted too, resting for the effort, reserving the remnants of energy left in my wearied muscles.

An unforgettable moment. I crept again, inching a way forward, snout of the gun grasped in my hand. The fellow turned a split second too late. The butt crashed. He gave a choking sort of grunt and crumpled up. A swift glance to right and left, then I was dragging him across the top of the wall—a matter of seven or eight feet and no light task, for he was a hefty wallah. I tumbled him over, heard the soft bump of his fall, and flopped over on top of him.

The drop took the breath out of me for a space. But soon I was up, scurrying off at a staggering run, heading blindly into the welcome darkness. Free! But was I? Dawn would soon be up now. There would come search-parties, scouring the countryside. In this land of fantastic hills and black gulleys, however, there were thousands of crevices in which one might hide. Soon I would lie down and sleep in some hideout of the gulley. I had to keep on telling myself that. It needed superhuman effort to keep moving just then.

I was still stumbling over the stones when the dawn broke up the black dome of the heavens. The village was a mere smudge away up on the hillside. I knew this gulley. It was the one through which a treacherous native servant had led me. I passed the identical cave in which I had lain hidden while my "boy"—every Indian servant is a boy, no matter what his age— had gone off as a decoy to lead the Mad Fakir back to me. But the boy had turned traitor. He not only brought Lenhai to my cave but a score of armed hillmen as well.

The plan was, of course, that the Mad Fakir should be induced to visit me alone, with the pretence that I had brought much valuable information about the sahibs of the Kurram Militia—otherwise Hell's Broth Militia, as it was so aptly nick-named. The scheme had flopped horribly. Hence my capture and subsequent torture.

No good dwelling on that now. Probably this cave was the last place they'd look in for me, since I had already been caught

118

there; but I gave it a wide berth just the same. I plodded on, careering crazily along the broken bed of the gulley. Now the sun was splashing the heavens with colour. Back in that village the hue and cry would be on. My world of rocks was turning from black to grey. A raging thirst was added to my other aches and pains. There must be something pretty tough about the instinct of self-preservation—otherwise I should have dropped in my tracks long ago.

I kept on, lurching over the broken stones like a sleep-walker. I knew by the sun that my direction was right. There wasn't a sound in that grim valley, except the stubbing of my clumsy feet against the flints. Then I pitched forward, lay still for a timeless period. Presently I began to crawl. I'd seen a ledge of rock that looked as if it contained water. Water! God in heaven! What thirst was this? It blistered my mouth. It threatened the breathing—as if one were about to choke.

But I made the ledge and I was right. I dragged myself along and lay with my head in the dirty water. The relief was indescribable. I drew in copious draughts of the cooling liquid, splashed it about head and neck. It might have been reeking with germs —probably was—but it was heaven-sent nectar to me! I lay drinking and bathing while my spirits rose. I could go on again now. I went, treading a rugged path along the hillside with leaden feet. I refused to give in to the creeping sensation of numbness. Arms hung like dead weights so that I hardly knew they were there. Only my legs seemed to move ... lurching, stumbling, pitching ... Then the blackout ...

I was not conscious of anything for the remainder of that day. I know that I awoke on one occasion and the whole world was dark. Night again, I thought feebly, and wondered just where I had fallen. Maybe I was on some perilous perch of rock. It was impossible to see in that dense blackness. Maybe some little movement would pitch me over on to jagged crags. Anyway, I was too utterly weary to move. The cool stone against the heated lacerations was infinitely soothing. I curled up and went to sleep again.

119

From then on—a fitful sleeping and dreams. Always when I awoke and opened my eyes the world was black, and for a space terror walked the brain. I fancied I must be blind. Why was it always dark? It was many hours before I realised that I must have crawled into the inner recess of a cave in the mountain-side. I had begun by groping my way around until I came to the shaft of light. Then I knew. Proceeding cautiously, I came to the mouth, and broad daylight. Whether I had been in that cleft one day or two I could not say. I was considerably refreshed. The flesh wound had crusted over. The broken thumb had swollen to the size of two. The ant-bites were not nearly so troublesome. I'd been a great deal nearer to death. As my brain grew clearer I saw that this was definitely a case for optimism.

I crawled out and gazed up and down the valley. It was a dead world. There was not a sign of life anywhere. So, I had escaped? How long would it take the company to locate me? They had not the remotest idea as to the direction the boy and I were to take. The whole thing was carried out with the utmost secrecy. It was only after much persuasion that the Colonel had permitted me to undertake the job at all. He had not reckoned on the treacherous native boy.

The rank and file of Hell's Broth Militia was composed entirely of natives, also the non-commissioned officers, with only half a dozen sahibs to control them. They were irregulars, many of whom claimed unbroken descent from the warriors who had fought the armies of Alexander the Great, others were just hard-bitten children of a mixed refugee parenthood of Afghans, Mongolians, Afridis, Pathan deserters, and heaven knows what. The force was composed of the worst native elements—cattle thieves, outlaws, bandits, deserters from the clans, and deserters from the Army proper—a strange brotherhood held together by a handful of officers, its chief industry guerilla fighting such as these rascals' forebears had enjoyed for centuries. As ferocious and wild a mob as any border country could muster.

But it was rare that we found a traitor amongst them. The pay and rationing were better than they could get elsewhere, and, more important still to natives of such calibre, there was always a scrap in the offing. Once they had adjusted themselves to our apology for discipline they were loyal almost to a man, despite their wildness. I could have staked my reputation on that native boy, for we had been on similar stunts before. Now I could only assume that he had turned traitor, since, having betrayed me to the Mad Fakir and his bodyguard, he had disappeared.

I thought hard of these things as I stared up and down that barren gully. How long since I left the camp? More than a week, I judged. Perhaps two. I was conscious of hunger and thirst, and I guess I must have been in that cave two or three days, maybe more. The company might search for weeks in this Free Land of the Hills without ever coming upon me. There were thousands of crannies and clefts in these regions where a man could lose himself. I could hardly hope for help in that direction. There was nothing for it but to make my own way back. If I kept going in a southerly direction I was almost certain to hit a caravan road and maybe a friendly caravan loping towards Peshawar with merchandise from Kabul or Bokhara.

I started out once more, trudging mechanically with a wary eye on the sun. It seemed as if I had the whole world to myself, and it appeared that way for hours. I struck a caravan trail at long last. It must then have been well past noon. I came upon a water-hole and sat down to refresh myself. I had no intention of falling asleep, but it is fatal for a weary man to sit drowsing in the sun.

I awoke with a jerk and leapt to my feet. Instinctively I struck out at the great hulking hillman who had awakened me. And then I had another guess coming. The fellow grabbed my arms, pinned them helplessly to my sides and held me thus. We stared at each other for long seconds. He looked a typical hillman—six feet of brawn and muscle, heavy, bearded jowl, damnably familiar in his turban, long tight-fitting coat, rough blouse, cummerbund, and baggy breeches. And then the shock of my life.

"Now . . . just where in hell did you spring from, buddy?"

This must be another delusion, I told myself. Here was a native of the mountains, every inch of him, clothes, stature, jowl, cartridge belts, guns, knives and all. And he was addressing me in English—English with American idioms and an Irish drawl! No. It couldn't be. Not in the middle of this country of black hills and grey stone. After all I'd gone through ... It was just my brain playing tricks on me ...

"Say that again," I gasped.

He grinned, showing two rows of even white teeth, big teeth, big like himself, big like tombstones in the black scrub of beard. He repeated the words, realising perhaps from my torn and ragged apology for a uniform that I'd been in some tough spot, repeated them slowly and carefully, his grey eyes twinkling.

"It's a long story. It cannot be told to any stranger who happens along. I'm trying to make my way back to the Kurram Militia cantonment. What excites me is just where *you* sprang from?"

"That's simple enough," the stranger laughed. "I'm trekking from Afghanistan to India. Been visiting Kabul. Which accounts for the native clobber I'm wearing. That's my caravan over there."

I swung round, stared hard. There, not fifty yards away, was a camel caravan replete with camelteers, baggage, water-skins, and all the usual paraphernalia of this ancient type of transport. Funny. I'd been too sound asleep to hear it approach, and too startled and excited at the encounter with this mysterious Irish-American to notice it after I had been so rudely awakened. I started laughing like a hysterical schoolgirl.

From Pretoria to the Sea

by JOHN BUCHAN

On November 15, 1899, Lieutenant-General Sir Aylmer Haldane, who in the Great War commanded the VI Corps, was thirty-seven years of age and a captain in the Gordon Highlanders. Mr Winston Churchill, who was afterwards to hold most offices in the British Cabinet, was then twenty-five, and was acting as correspondent for the *Morning Post* on the Natal front. He had already seen service with his regiment, the 4th Hussars, on the Indian frontier, and in other capacities in Cuba and on the Nile. The South African War had just begun, and so far had gone badly for Britain. Sir George White was cut off in Ladysmith; but Sir Redvers Buller had landed in Natal, and it was believed that he would soon advance to an easy victory.

The South African War, as we all know, was entered upon light-heartedly and with very scanty fore-knowledge of the problems to be faced. Much of the British equipment was amateurish; but the palm for amateurishness must be given to the armoured train which plied its trade in the neighbourhood of Estcourt. It was not much better than a death-trap. It was made up of an engine, five wagons, and an ancient 7-pounder muzzle-loading gun. Its purpose was reconnaissance; but it was a very noisy and conspicuous scout, as it wheezed up and down the line, belching clouds of smoke and steam.

On the morning of 15th November it set out to reconnoitre towards Chieveley, carrying on board 120 men, made up of a small civilian breakdown gang, part of a company of the Dublin Fusiliers, and a company of the Durban Light Infantry Volunteers. Captain Haldane was in command, and Mr Churchill, in his capacity as a War Correspondent, went with him. When they reached Chieveley, Boer horsemen were observed, and the train was ordered back to Frere. But before it reached Frere it was discovered that a hill commanding the whole line at a distance of 600 yards was occupied by the enemy.

The driver put on full steam and tried to run the gauntlet, but a big stone had been placed on the line at the foot of a steep gradient, and into this the train crashed. The engine, which was in the centre of the train, was not derailed, and a gallant attempt was made to clear the wreckage of the foremost trucks and push through. For more than an hour, under heavy shell-fire from the enemy's field guns, and a constant hail of rifle bullets, the crew of the train laboured to clear the obstruction. But the couplings of the trucks broke, and though the engine, laden with wounded, managed to continue its journey, the position of the rest of the crew was hopeless, and they were compelled to surrender. The Boers behaved with conspicuous humanity, and the little company of prisoners were soon jogging slowly northward towards Pretoria.

The capital of the then South African Republic was a little new town planned in orderly parallelograms lying in a cup among rocky hills. From it three railways radiated—one to Pietersburg and the north, one to Johannesburg in the south-west, and one running eastward to Portuguese territory and the sea at Delagoa Bay. The British privates and non-commissioned officers were sent to a camp at the racecourse on the outskirts of the town, while the officers were taken to the Staats Model School, a building almost in the centre of Pretoria. At first Mr Churchill was sent with the men, but he was presently brought back and added to the officers. He bore a name which was better known than liked in the Transvaal at the time, and his presence as a prisoner was a considerable satisfaction to his captors.

The Staats Model School was a single-storied red-brick building with a slated veranda, and consisted of twelve classrooms, a large lecture hall, and a gymnasium. The playground, in which it stood, was about 120 yards square, and in it there were tents for the guards, the cookhouse and a bathing-shed. On two sides it was surrounded by an iron grill, and on the other two by a corrugated iron fence some 10 feet high. Before the prisoners from the armoured train arrived there were already sixty British officers there, captured in the early Natal fighting. For guard there were twenty-seven men and three corporals of the South African Republic Police (known locally as "Zarps"). These furnished nine sentries in reliefs of four hours; they stood 50 yards apart, well armed with revolvers and rifles. In every street of Pretoria, too, were posted special armed constables.

To be taken prisoner thus early, in what was believed to be a triumphant war, was a bitter pill for British officers to swallow, and it was not easier for the restless, energetic spirit of Mr Churchill. As soon as the captives arrived they began to make plans for escape. None of them was on parole, and at first sight it looked a comparatively easy task. It would not be hard to scale the flimsy outer defences of the Staats Model School, but the trouble lay in the guards. It was found impossible to bribe them, for, as Mr Churchill has observed in his book, the presence of so many millionaires in the country had raised the tariff too high for any ordinary purse. Another difficulty was where to go. It was no good attempting to reach Natal or Cape Colony, for that meant going through Boer armies. The best chance lay eastward in the direction of Portuguese territory, but that involved a journey of 300 miles through an unknown country. The one hope was the Delagoa Bay line, for where there is a railway there are always chances of transport for a bold man.

Captain Haldane's mind turned to tunnelling, and he discovered in an old cupboard several screwdrivers and wire-cutters, which he managed to secrete. Mr Churchill had a more

125

audacious plan. He observed that the sentries on the side of the quadrangle remote from the road were at certain times, as they walked on their beats, unable to see the top of a few yards of the boundary wall. There were brilliant electric lights in the middle of the quadrangle, but the sentries beyond them could not see very well what lay behind. If it were possible to pass the two sentries on that side at the exact moment when both their backs were turned together, the wall might be scaled and the garden of the villa next door reached. Beyond that it was impossible to plan. Mr Churchill and a friend resolved to make the attempt and to trust to the standing luck of the British Army to get safely out of the town and cover the 280 miles to the Portuguese border. They had a fair amount of money, they would carry some chocolate with them, and they hoped to buy mealies at the native kraals. They knew no Kafir or Dutch, and would have to lie hidden by day and move only in the darkness.

The enterprise was fixed for the night of 11th December, and was to be attempted at seven o'clock when the bell rang for dinner. The two spent a nervous afternoon; but when the bell rang it was seen that the thing was hopeless. The sentries did not walk about, and one stood opposite the one climbable part of the wall. "With a most unsatisfactory feeling of relief" the two went to bed. The next evening came and again the dinner bell rang. Mr Churchill walked across the quadrangle, and from a corner in one of the offices watched the sentries. After half an hour one suddenly turned and walked up to his comrade and began to talk. The chance had come. Mr Churchill ran to the wall, pulled himself up, and lay flat on the top while the sentries with their backs turned were talking 15 yards away. Then he dropped into the shrubs of the garden.

It was a night of full moonlight, but there was fair cover in the bushes. The villa to which the garden belonged was 20 yards off, and the undrawn curtains revealed brightly lighted windows with figures moving about. Mr Churchill had to wait for the arrival of his comrade, and as he waited a man came out of the back door of the villa and walked in his direction across the garden. Ten yards away he stopped and appeared to be watching, while the fugitive remained absolutely still with a thumping heart. Then another man joined the first, lit a cigar, and the two walked off together. Then a cat was pursued by a dog, rushed into the bushes, and collided with the fugitive. The two men stopped, but, reflecting that it was only the cat, passed out of the garden gate into the town.

Mr Churchill had now been lying there an hour, when he heard a voice from inside the quadrangle say quite loud, "All up!" He crawled back to the wall and heard two officers walking up and down talking. One of them mentioned his name. He coughed; one of the officers thereupon began to chatter some kind of nonsense while the other said slowly, "He cannot get out. The sentry suspects. It is all up. Can you get back again?" But to go back was impossible, and though Mr Churchill had very little hope he determined to have a run for his money. He said loudly and clearly, so that the others heard him, "I shall go on alone!"

The first thing was to get out of Pretoria. He had managed during his confinement to acquire a suit of dark clothes, different from the ordinary garments issued to prisoners. To reach the road he must pass a sentry at short range, but he decided that the boldest course was the safest. He got up, walked past the windows of the villa, passed the sentry at less than 50 yards, and, after walking 100 yards and hearing no challenge, knew that he had surmounted the second obstacle.

It was a queer experience to be at large on a bright moonlight night in the heart of the enemy's capital, nearly 300 miles from friendly territory, and with a certainty that in an hour or two there would be a hue and cry out against him. He strolled at a leisurely pace down the middle of the streets, humming a tune, past crowds of burghers, till he reached the environs. There he sat down and reflected. His escape would probably not be known till dawn, and he must get some way off before daybreak, for all the neighbouring country would be patrolled. He had £ 75 in his pocket and four slabs of chocolate, but the compass, map, opium tablets, and meat lozenges were left behind with his unlucky friend. His only chance was the Delagoa Bay Railway. That line, of course, was guarded, and every train would be searched; but among a multitude of black alternatives it gave at least one ray of hope.

Half a mile later he struck the railroad, but he could not be sure whether it was the Pietersburg or the Delagoa Bay line, for it appeared to run north instead of east. He followed it, and soon began to realize the exhilaration of escape. Walking in the cool night under the stars his spirits rose. There were pickets along the line and watchers at every bridge, but he avoided them all by short detours. And as he walked he reflected that if he trusted to his feet to cover the 300 miles he would very soon be captured. He must make better speed, and the only chance for that was a train. Yes, a train must be boarded, and at the earliest possible opportunity.

When he had walked for two hours he perceived the lights of a station, so he left the track and hid in a ditch 200 yards beyond the buildings. He argued that any train would stop at the station and by the time it reached him would not have got up much speed. After another hour he heard a train whistle and saw the yellow headlights of the engine. It waited five minutes in the station, and then, with a great rumbling, started again. Mr Churchill flung himself on the trucks, got some sort of handhold, and with a great struggle seated himself on the couplings. It was a goods train, and the trucks were full of empty sacks covered with coal dust, among which he burrowed. He had no notion whether or not he was on the right line, and he was too tired to worry, so he simply fell asleep. He woke before daybreak and realised that he must leave the train ere dawn. So he sat himself again on the couplings, and, catching hold of the iron handle at the back of the truck, sprang to the side. The next moment he was sprawling in a ditch, much shaken but not hurt.

He found himself in the middle of a valley surrounded by low hills. Presently the dawn began to break, and to his relief he realised that he had taken the right railway. The line ran straight

128

into the sunrise. He had a long drink from a pool, and resolved to select a hiding-place to lie up for the day. This he found in a patch of wood on the side of a deep ravine, where, in the company of a cynical vulture, he spent the daylight hours. From his eyrie he could see a little tin-roofed town in the west, through which he had passed in the night, and in the immediate neighbourhood farmsteads with clumps of trees. There was a Kafir kraal at the bottom of the hill, and he watched the natives drive the flocks of goats and cows to the pastures. His only food was one slab of chocolate, which produced a violent thirst; but, as the water pool was half a mile away in the open and men were constantly passing, he dare not risk going for a drink.

His prospects were pretty black when he started again at the first darkness. He had a drink from the pool, and then took to the railway line in hope of getting a second train ride. But no train came, and for six hours in the bright moonlight he walked on, avoiding the Kafirs' huts and the guarded bridges. When he had to make a circuit he fell into bogs, and, as he was in a poor condition from the previous month's imprisonment, he was very soon tired out.

Mr Churchill published the story of his escape during the war, when it was important not to implicate any friends still in the Transvaal, and so the next part of his journey has never been explicitly told. It appears that he fell in with a Mr Burnham and a Mr Howard, officials of a colliery, who gave him valuable assistance, as they were afterwards to assist Captain Haldane. On the fifth day after leaving Pretoria he reached Middelburg, where it was arranged that he should try and board a Delagoa Bay train.

Meantime the hue and cry was out against him. Telegrams describing him at great length were sent along every railway; 3,000 photographs were printed, and warrants were issued for his immediate arrest. Officials of the prison who knew him by sight hurried off to Komati Poort, the frontier stations, to examine travellers. It was rumoured that he had escaped disguised as a woman, and again disguised as a policeman; and finally it was reported that he was still in hiding in Pretoria. The Dutch news-

129

papers considered it a sinister fact that just before he escaped he had become a subscriber to the State Library and had borrowed Mill's *On Liberty!*

On the sixth day he found a train to Delagoa Bay standing in a siding, which he boarded. The journey should take not more than thirty-six hours, so the provisions carried were not elaborate, and he had only one bottle of water. He managed to ensconce himself in a truck laden with great sacks of some soft merchandise, and worm his way to the bottom. The heat was stifling, for it was midsummer in the Transvaal, and the floor of the truck was littered with coal dust, which did not add to its amenities.

These last days of the adventure were both anxious and uncomfortable. He scarcely dared to sleep for fear of snoring, and he was in terror that at Komati Poort, the frontier station of the Transvaal, the trucks would be searched. His anxiety there was prolonged, for the train was shunted for eighteen hours on to a siding. Indeed, his truck was actually searched, and the upper tarpaulin was removed, but the police were careless and did not search deep enough.

At length, two and a half days after he left Middelburg, and eight and a half days from Pretoria, the train crawled into Delagoa Bay. Mr Churchill emerged from his hole in the last stages of dirt, hunger, and weariness. But all troubles were now past. He went first to the British consul, who thought he was a fireman from one of the ships in the harbour, and who welcomed him with enthusiasm when he learned his real name. Clothes were bought; he had a long wash, and at last a civilized meal. That very night, as it happened, a steamer was leaving for Durban, and in case any of the Boer agents at Delagoa Bay should attempt to recapture him, some dozen of the English residents, armed with revolvers, escorted him on board. A few days later Mr Churchill was back again in Natal with the British Army.

We return to Captain Haldane and his friends, who had been meditating escape from the first day of their arrival at the Staats Model School. The difficulty was, of course, the guards, and

"The upper tarpaulin was removed, but the police were
careless and did not search deep enough."

Mr Churchill's exploit made the Boer Government redouble its vigilance. It was found impossible to bribe the sentries; a plan for a rising of the prisoners was soon given up; and the scheme of sinking a shaft and then tunnelling to an adjacent kitchen garden proved impracticable, since the diggers very soon struck water. For three miserable months Captain Haldane cogitated in vain, and the best he could do was to get hold of a tourist map of South Africa and study the country east of Pretoria in case some way of escape should present itself. Meantime an incident cheered the prisoners. A man accompanied by a St Bernard dog took to walking outside the school and signalling by the Morse code with his stick. He was warned off by the guards, but he found another means of communication and sent messages from an adjacent house giving the news of the war.

In the middle of February 1900 there was a rumour that the officers were to be moved to a new building from which escape would be impossible. This gave Captain Haldane an idea. He resolved to go into hiding beneath the floor, so that the Boers should think he had escaped, and then, when the officers were moved and the building was left empty, to emerge and get out of the town. His companions in the attempt were Lieutenant Neil Le Mesurier of the Dublin Fusiliers and Sergeant-Major A. Brockie of the Imperial Light Horse. They collected a few necessary articles, opened the trap-door, and went to earth.

It was a horrible place in which they found themselves. The floor of the building was about $2\frac{1}{2}$ feet above the ground, and the space below was divided into five narrow compartments by four stone walls, on which the cross beams rested. Each of these compartments was about 18 feet long and $3\frac{1}{2}$ feet wide, and there were manholes between them. The air, what there was of it, came through a small ventilator somewhere on the veranda. The place was pitch dark, and the atmosphere was stuffy to the last degree.

The three thought that their imprisonment there would only last for twenty-four hours. They went to earth on 26th February, and next day there was a great to-do about their disappearance.

132

Descriptions of them were circulated over the whole country. One of their friends above, Lieutenant Frankland of the Dublin Fusiliers, arranged a small daily supply of provisions. Alas! the twenty-four hours passed and there was no move above. For nineteen days the three men remained in that horrible dungeon. Their only exercise was crawling about, in which they broke their heads constantly against beams and walls. They were covered with dirt, for very little water could be passed through the trap-door. Still they managed to endure. By the light of a dip they played games of patience and talked, and their chief anxiety was lest by snoring or talking in their sleep they should give their hiding-place away. Their friends above who were in the secret tried to persuade them to come up occasionally to get some fresh air, but they were determined to play the game according to its rigour, and refused.

But the situation was getting serious, for all three were falling ill. Captain Haldane wrote to a fellow-prisoner in the school above, a Dutch pastor called Adrian Hofmeyer, begging him to try and get the move expedited. Hofmeyer did his best with the authorities, telling them the story of a bogus rising of the prisoners; but still nothing happened. At last came the good news that the move was fixed for Friday, 16th March. The prisoners underground heard the commandant going his rounds for the last time. Then their friends gave the agreed signal, and Frankland's voice said, "Good-bye". At a quarter-past ten the prisoners were heard leaving the school, and by midday the servants and baggage had left. The three stayed below till nightfall and then walked out of the empty building. Walking is, indeed, a misnomer, for they seemed to have lost the use of their legs. They fell repeatedly and reeled like drunken men. It was not till they had got out of the town that they recovered the use of their limbs.

They had 300 miles of a difficult journey to make to safety, and surely never in the history of escapes have three men started out on a wilder enterprise in worse physical condition. Mr Churchill had been out of training, but his physique at the time was that of an athlete's compared to Captain Haldane and his companions.

133

Brockie, who had lived in the country and knew the language, got himself up like a wounded Boer, with his left arm in a sling and the Boer colours round his head. The trio presented the appearance of the worst kind of Irish moonlighters.

In the suburbs a special constable looked at them suspiciously, but was reassured by the sight of Brockie's wounded arm. They struck the Delagoa Bay Railway and stumbled along it, Le Mesurier having the bad luck to sprain his ankle. Their one advantage was that, having been supposed to escape three weeks before, the immediate hue and cry after them had died down.

Their first halting-place was near a station on the line, 13 miles east of Pretoria. There they lay up, suffering much from mosquitoes, and when darkness came made for the highroad running east. The Transvaal highways at that time were not like those of to-day, but simply raw red scars running across the veld, by no means easy to follow in the darkness. On this second night of their travels they were hunted by dogs, and Haldane and Le Mesurier took refuge in a stream, cowering up to their necks. Here they lost Brockie, but fortunately he was the one of the three best able to fend for himself, as he knew the country and could speak both Dutch and Kafir. The two, soaked to the skin, spent the rest of the night in a clump of bracken, after taking a dose of quinine and opium. At daybreak they found themselves stiff with rheumatism. They had finished their whisky, and the provisions, matches, and tobacco were soaked.

At dawn, in a tremendous thunderstorm, they made for the railway again, and there Haldane, to his consternation, discovered that he had left his money and belt in the last hiding-place. He dared not return for them, even if he had had any hope of finding the place again. So there were the two men, without food or money, weary, cramped, and sick, with the better part of 300 miles before them in an enemy country.

Food must be found, and that night they came on a Kafir kraal with a field of water melons. They made a meal off the melons and stumbled on again. The next night their physical condition began to be really serious. In four nights they had only covered

134

36 miles, and their food was reduced to one tin of pemmican, one tin of cocoa, and a scrap of biltong. They had hoped for mealies from the fields, but the mealie harvest had just been gathered and not a cob remained. Another misfortune was the condition of the veld grass. They had expected it to be long enought to hide in, but it was far too short for shelter, and they were therefore compelled to lie up by day in wet swamps.

That night, having finished every scrap of food, they blundered into a Kafir hut beside a coal siding, where some natives were eating mealiemeal porridge. Their only course was to reveal themselves, for the Kafirs were in the main on the British side. They learned that the natives' master, the manager of the coal mine, was a Dane, and to him they disclosed their identity. The manager was friendly. He said his own mine was sending no coals to the coast for the moment, but that at a colliery next door three trucks were being loaded up for Delagoa Bay next morning. He handed his visitors over to the storekeeper of the mine, Mr Moore, who gave them a dry bed and a good meal.

Next morning they heard that the mine doctor, a Scotsman called Gillespie, was coming to see them, and in him they found a stout ally, for he knew all about their escape and had been looking for their arrival in order to help them. He was one of the people who had already assisted Mr Churchill. That evening he undertook to drive them to another mine, where a plan of escape could be matured.

In the early darkness they drove 14 miles over the veld to the colliery of the Transvaal Delagoa Bay Company. There they were handed over to Mr J. E. Howard, who had been the chief agent in Mr Churchill's escape. There, too, they were introduced to Mr Addams, the secretary of the mine, who turned out to be no other than the Englishman with the St Bernard dog who had been accustomed to walk past the Staats Model School. He and the manager of the mine store, Mr Burnham, at once set about planning their escape. It was arranged that Mr Howard should feign illness for a few days and remain indoors, and that Hal-

135

dane and Le Mesurier should take up their quarters with him. To their relief they also got news of Brockie, for he had turned up a little earlier at the same place and had been given a passport to the border.

The plan arranged was as follows: wool was still being sent down from the high veld to Delagoa Bay, and the trucks for it were usually detached at Middelburg. It was arranged that Burnham should buy a truckload of wool and wire to a firm at Delagoa Bay offering the consignment. This was done, wires were exchanged, and sixteen bales of wool were duly collected and consigned to the coast. The truck for the wool was brought up the line and carefully loaded. The bales, each of which weighed 400 lb., were so arranged that there was a kind of tunnel at the bottom down the centre, in which the fugitives could hide. From behind the blinds in the sickroom of Mr Howard, Haldane and Le Mesurier watched with acute interest the last stages of these preparations.

At 5 a.m. one morning they climbed into the tunnel below the wool, where their friends had provided them with ample provisions for a week in the shape of roast duck and chicken, beef and bread, butter and jam, nine bottles of cold tea, two of water, and one of whisky. The tarpaulin was made fast over the top, and for five hours the two waited. At ten o'clock that morning Mr Howard came along and took a final farewell. A certain Field-Cornet Pretorius had arrived that morning and had shown himself very suspicious about the tablecloth in Mr Howard's dining-room, but the manager had explained it with the story of a dinner and card party. By midday the truck was taken by a colliery engine to Whitbank station. Mr Addams and Mr Burnham were on the lookout there, and to their horror saw the Dutch driver and stoker stroll up and lean against the truck. They endeavoured to draw them away by offers of drinks; but the driver would not move, and taking a paper from his pocket began to conduct his correspondence against the side of the truck. A sneeze or a word from inside would have given away the whole plan. Even when the man left the danger was not over, for while the truck was being shunted, one of the station officials actually undid the tarpaulin and looked in, but saw nothing.

At 2.30 p.m. they were attached to a passenger train, and for the rest of the day jogged across the high veld, till at Waterval Boven, where the descent to the low veld begins, the train drew up for the night. They started again next morning, and presently they reached the last Transvaal station, Komati Poort, where a bridge spans the Komati river. This was the place where a search was likely, and to the intense disappointment of the fugitives they found the truck detached and pushed into a siding. Discovery seemed now certain, and Haldane decided to try and bribe the first comer. He got a bag of a hundred sovereigns ready, and destroyed any compromising matter in his diary.

As it happened, the Pretoria Government had wired to Komati Poort to order the strictest search of all goods trucks. The stowaways heard the unloosening of the ropes of their tarpaulin, and down in their tunnel realised it had been lifted up and thrown back. They saw daylight flood in at the tunnel end, and believed that any moment the face of a station official would look down on them. Then to their amazement the tarpaulin was returned to its place. They may not have been seen; or a Kafir may have caught a glimpse of them, and, having no desire to aid the law, said nothing.

But though the tarpaulin was drawn again, their suspense was not over. All that day and all the following night they lay there, anxious, half stifled, and now very hungry, for they had thrown away most of their provisions, believing that they would not be needed. Saturday morning came, and they realised that they had hoped the day before to be inside the Portuguese border. At last, at 9 a.m., the train steamed off, and while crossing the Komati bridge the two men shook hands. They saw the white pillar which marked the boundary, and realised that they had won freedom.

The train stopped at the first Portuguese station; but the two stowaways did not dare to alight. They waited till the evening and then crept out in the dusk. At a Kafir kraal close by they

"*While crossing the Komati bridge the two men shook hands.*"

learned that the hotel there was kept by two Englishmen, and thither they stumbled. In five minutes they were in a back room being regaled with champagne by their excited compatriots.

Brockie had also escaped, but all three paid for some time the penalty of their wild adventure with malaria, and in the case of Le Mesurier with enteric. In a few weeks, however, they were back on duty at the front. Captain Haldane, as we have seen, was to rise to be one of the most successful British generals in the Great War. Brockie was killed by a mining accident a few years after the escape. Le Mesurier fell at the Second Battle of Ypres, and Frankland, who had assisted them to escape, died in a reconnaissance at the Dardanelles.

The Speckled Band

by SIR ARTHUR CONAN DOYLE

In glancing over my notes of the seventy-odd cases in which I have during the last eight years studied the methods of my friend Sherlock Holmes, I find many tragic, some comic, a large number merely strange, but none commonplace; for, working as he did rather for the love of his art than for the acquirement of wealth, he refused to associate himself with any investigation which did not tend towards the unusual, and even the fantastic. Of all these varied cases, however, I cannot recall any which presented more singular features than that which was associated with the well-known Surrey family of the Roylotts of Stoke Moran. The events in question occurred in the early days of my association with Holmes, when we were sharing rooms as bachelors, in Baker Street. It is possible that I might have placed them upon record before, but a promise of secrecy was made at the time, from which I have only been freed during the last month by the untimely death of the lady to whom the pledge was given. It is perhaps as well that the facts should now come to light, for I have reasons to know there are widespread rumours as to the death of Dr Grimesby Roylott, which tend to make the matter even more terrible than the truth.

It was early in April, in the year '83, that I woke one morning to find Sherlock Holmes standing, fully dressed, by the side of my bed. He was a late riser as a rule, and, as the clock on the mantel-piece showed me that it was only a quarter past seven, I blinked up at him in some surprise, and perhaps just a little resentment, for I was myself regular in my habits.

"Very sorry to knock you up, Watson," said he, "but it's the common lot this morning. Mrs Hudson has been knocked up; she retorted upon me, and I on you."

"What is it, then? A fire?"

"No, a client. It seems that a young lady has arrived in a considerable state of excitement, who insists upon seeing me. She is waiting now in the sitting-room. Now, when young ladies wander about the Metropolis at this hour of the morning, and knock sleepy people up out of their beds, I presume that it is something very pressing which they have to communicate. Should it prove to be an interesting case, you would, I am sure, wish to follow it from the outset. I thought at any rate that I should call you, and give you the chance."

"My dear fellow, I would not miss it for anything."

I had no keener pleasure than in following Holmes in his professional investigations, and in admiring the rapid deductions, as swift as intuitions, and yet always founded on a logical basis, with which he unravelled the problems which were submitted to him. I rapidly threw on my clothes, and was ready in a few minutes to accompany my friend down to the sitting-room. A lady dressed in black and heavily veiled, who had been sitting in the window, rose as we entered.

"Good morning, madam," said Holmes cheerily. "My name is Sherlock Holmes. This is my intimate friend and associate, Dr Watson, before whom you can speak freely as before myself. Ha, I am glad to see that Mrs Hudson has had the good sense to light the fire. Pray draw up to it, and I shall order you a cup of hot coffee, for I observe that you are shivering."

"It is not cold which makes me shiver," said the woman in a low voice, changing her seat as requested.

"What then?"

"It is fear, Mr Holmes. It is terror." She raised her veil as she

"A lady dressed in black and heavily veiled rose as we entered."

spoke, and we could see that she was indeed in a pitiable state of agitation, her face all drawn and grey, with restless, frightened eyes, like those of some hunted animal. Her features and figure were those of a woman of thirty, but her hair was shot with premature grey, and her expression was weary and haggard. Sherlock Holmes ran her over with one of his quick, allcomprehensive glances.

"You must not fear," said he soothingly, bending forward and patting her forearm. "We shall soon set matters right, I have no doubt. You have come in by train this morning, I see."

"You know me, then?"

"No, but I observe the second half of a return ticket in the palm of your left glove. You must have started early, and yet you had a good drive in a dog-cart, along heavy roads, before you reached the station."

The lady gave a violent start, and stared in bewilderment at my companion.

"There is no mystery, my dear madam," said he, smiling. "The left arm of your jacket is spattered with mud in no less than seven places. The marks are perfectly fresh. There is no vehicle save a dog-cart which throws up mud in that way, and then only when you sit on the left-hand side of the driver."

"Whatever your reasons may be, you are perfectly correct," said she. "I started from home before six, reached Leatherhead at twenty past, and came in by the first train to Waterloo. Sir, I can stand this strain no longer, I shall go mad if it continues. I have no one to turn to—none, save only one, who cares for me, and he, poor fellow, can be of little aid. I have heard of you Mr Holmes; I have heard of you from Mrs Farintosh, whom you helped in the hour of her sore need. It was from her that I had your address. Oh, sir, do you not think you could help me too, and at least throw a little light through the dense darkness which surrounds me? At present it is out of my power to reward you for your services, but in a month or two I shall be married, with the control of my own income, and then at least you shall not find me ungrateful."

Holmes turned to his desk, and unlocking it, drew out a small casebook which he consulted.

"Farintosh," said he. "Ah, yes, I recall the case; it was concerned with an opal tiara. I think it was before your time, Watson. I can only say, madam, that I shall be happy to devote the same care to your case as I did to that of your friend. As to reward, my profession is its reward; but you are at liberty to defray whatever expenses I may be put to, at the time which suits you best. And now I beg that you will lay before us everything that may help us in forming an opinion upon the matter."

"Alas!" replied our visitor. "The very horror of my situation lies in the fact that my fears are so vague, and my suspicions depend so entirely upon small points, which might seem trivial to another, that even he to whom of all others I have a right to look for help and advice looks upon all that I tell him about it as the fancies of a nervous woman. He does not say so, but I can read it from his soothing answers and averted eyes. But I have heard, Mr Holmes, that you can see deeply into the manifold wickedness of the human heart. You may advise me how to walk amid the dangers which encompass me."

"I am all attention, madam."

"My name is Helen Stoner, and I am living with my stepfather, who is the last survivor of one of the oldest Saxon families in England, the Roylotts of Stoke Moran, on the western border of Surrey."

Holmes nodded his head. "The name is familiar to me," said he.

"The family was at one time among the richest in England, and the estate extended over the borders into Berkshire in the north, and Hampshire in the west. In the last century, however, four successive heirs were of a dissolute and wasteful disposition, and the family ruin was eventually completed by a gambler, in the days of the Regency. Nothing was left save a few acres of ground and the two-hundred-year-old house, which is itself crushed under a heavy mortgage. The last squire dragged out his existence there, living the horrible life of an aristocrat pauper; but his only son, my stepfather, seeing that he must adapt himself to the new conditions, obtained an advance from a relative, which enabled him to take a medical degree, and went out to Calcutta, where, by his professional skill and his force of character, he established a large practice. In a fit of anger, however, caused by some robberies which had been perpetrated in the house, he beat his native butler to death, and narrowly escaped a capital sentence. As it was, he suffered a long term of imprisonment, and afterwards returned to England a morose and disappointed man.

"When Dr Roylott was in India he married my mother, Mrs Stoner, the young widow of Major-General Stoner, of the Bengal Artillery. My sister Julia and I were twins, and we were only two years old at the time of my mother's re-marriage. She had a considerable sum of money, not less that a thousand a year, and this she bequeathed to Dr Roylott entirely whilst we resided with him, with a provision that a certain annual sum should be allowed to each of us in the event of our marriage. Shortly after our return to England my mother died—she was killed eight years ago in a railway accident near Crewe. Dr Roylott then abandoned his attempts to establish himself in practice in London and took us to live with him in the ancestral house at Stoke Moran. The money which my mother had left was enough for all our wants, and there seemed no obstacle to our happiness.

"But a terrible change came over our stepfather about this time. Instead of our making friends and exchanging visits with our neighbours, who had at first been overjoyed to see a Roylott of Stoke Moran back in the old family seat, he shut himself up in his house, and seldom came out save to indulge in ferocious quarrels with whoever might cross his path. Violence of temper approaching to mania has been hereditary in the men of the family, and in my stepfather's case it had, I believe, been intensified by his long residence in the tropics. A series of disgraceful brawls took place, two of which ended in the police court, until at last he became the terror of the village, and the folks would fly at his approach, for he is a man of immense strength, and absolutely uncontrollable in his anger.

"Last week he hurled the local blacksmith over a parapet into a stream and it was only by paying over all the money that I could gather that I was able to avert another public exposure. He had no friends at all save the wandering gipsies, and he would give these vagabonds leave to encamp upon the few acres of bramble-covered land which represent the family estate, and would accept in return the hospitality of their tents, wandering away with them sometimes for weeks on end. He has a passion also for Indian animals, which are sent over to him by a correspondent, and he has at the moment a cheetah and a baboon, which wander freely over his grounds, and are feared by the villagers almost as much as their master.

"You can imagine from what I say that my poor sister Julia and I had no great pleasure in our lives. No servant would stay with us, and for a long time we did all the work of the house. She was but thirty at the time of her death, and yet her hair had already begun to whiten, even as mine has."

"Your sister is dead, then?"

"She died just two years ago, and it is of her death that I wish to speak to you. You can understand that, living the life which I have described, we were little likely to see anyone of our own age and position. We had, however, an aunt, my mother's maiden sister, Miss Honoria Westphail, who lives near Harrow, and we were occasionally allowed to pay short visits at this lady's house. Julia went there at Christmas two years ago, and met there a half-pay Major of Marines, to whom she became engaged. My step-father learned of the engagement when my sister returned, and offered no objection to the marriage; but within a fortnight of the day which had been fixed for the wedding, the terrible event occurred which has deprived me of my only companion."

Sherlock Holmes had been leaning back in his chair with his eyes closed, and his head sunk in a cushion, but he half opened his lids now, and glanced across at this visitor.

"Pray be precise as to details," said he.

"It is easy for me to be so, for every event of that dreadful time is seared into my memory. The manor house is, as I have already said, very old, and only one wing is now inhabited. The bedrooms

146

in this wing are on the ground floor, the sitting-rooms being in the central block of the buildings. Of these bedrooms, the first is Dr Roylott's, the second my sister's and the third my own. There is no communication between them, but they all open out into the same corridor. Do I make myself plain?"

"Perfectly so."

"The windows of the three rooms open out upon the lawn. That fatal night Dr Roylott had gone to his room early, though we knew that he had not retired to rest, for my sister was troubled by the smell of the strong Indian cigars which it was his custom to smoke. She left her room, therefore, and came into mine, where she sat for some time, chatting about her approaching wedding. At eleven o'clock she rose to leave me, but she paused at the door and looked back.

"Tell me, Helen," said she, "have you ever heard anyone whistle in the dead of night?"

"Never," said I.

"I suppose that you could not possibly whistle yourself in your sleep?"

"Certainly not. But why?"

"Because during the last few nights I have always, about three in the morning, heard a low, clear whistle. I am a light sleeper, and it has awakened me. I cannot tell where it came from—perhaps from the next room, perhaps from the lawn. I thought that I would just ask you whether you had heard it."

"No, I have not. It must be those wretched gipsies in the plantation."

"Very likely. And yet if it were on the lawn I wonder that you did not hear it also."

"Ah, but I sleep more heavily than you."

"Well, it is of no great consequence at any rate." She smiled back at me, closed my door, and a few moments later I heard her key turn in the lock."

"Indeed," said Holmes. "Was it your custom always to lock yourselves in at night?"

"Always."

147

"And why?"

"I think that I mentioned to you that the Doctor kept a cheetah and a baboon. We had no feeling of security unless our doors were locked."

"Quite so. Pray proceed with your statement."

"I could not sleep that night. A vague feeling of impending misfortune impressed me. My sister and I, you will recollect, were twins, and you know how subtle are the links which bind two souls which are so closely allied. It was a wild night. The wind was howling outside, and the rain was beating and splashing against the windows. Suddenly, amidst all the hubbub of the gale, there burst forth the wild scream of a terrified woman. I knew that it was my sister's voice. I sprang from my bed, wrapped a shawl round me, and rushed into the corridor. As I opened my door I seemed to hear a low whistle, such as my sister described, and a few moments later a clanging sound, as if a mass of metal had fallen. As I ran down the passage my sister's door was unlocked, and revolved slowly upon its hinges. I stared at it horror-stricken, not knowing what was about to issue from it. By the light of the corridor lamp I saw my sister appear at the opening, her face blanched with terror, her hands groping for help, her whole figure swaying to and fro like that of a drunkard. I ran to her and threw my arms round her, but at that moment her knees seemed to give way and she fell to the ground. She writhed as one who is in terrible pain, and her limbs were dreadfully convulsed. At first I thought that she had not recognised me, but as I bent over her she suddenly shrieked out in a voice which I shall never forget, 'O, my God! Helen! It was the band! The speckled band!' There was something else which she would fain have said, and she stabbed with her finger into the air in the direction of the Doctor's room, but a fresh convulsion seized her and choked her words. I rushed out, calling loudly for my stepfather, and I met him hastening from his room in his dressing-gown. When he reached my sister's side she was unconscious, and though he poured brandy down her throat, and sent for medical aid from the village, all efforts were in vain, for she slowly sank and died without having recovered her consciousness. Such was the dreadful end of my beloved sister."

"One moment," said Holmes; "are you sure about this whistle and metallic sound? Could you swear to it?"

"That is what the county coroner asked me at the inquiry. It is my strong impression that I heard it, and yet among the crash of the gale, and the creaking of an old house, I may possibly have been deceived."

"Was your sister dressed?"

"No, she was in her nightdress. In her right hand was found the charred stump of a match, and in her left a matchbox."

"Showing that she had struck a light and looked about her when the alarm took place. That is important. And what conclusion did the coroner come to?"

"He investigated the case with great care, for Dr Roylott's conduct had long been notorious in the county, but he was unable to find any satisfactory cause of death. My evidence showed that the door had been fastened upon the inner side, and the windows were blocked by old-fashioned shutters with broad iron bars, which were secured every night. The walls were carefully sounded, and were shown to be quite solid all round, and the flooring was also thoroughly examined, with the same result. The chimney is wide, but is barred up by four large staples. It is certain, therefore, that my sister was quite alone when she met her end. Besides, there were no marks of any violence upon her."

"How about poison?"

"The doctors examined her for it, but without success."

"What do you think that this unfortunate lady died of, then?"

"It is my belief that she died of pure fear and nervous shock, though what it was which frightened her I cannot imagine."

"Were there gipsies in the plantation at the time?"

"Yes, there are nearly always some there."

"Ah, and what did you gather from this allusion to a band—a speckled band?"

"Sometimes I have thought that it was merely the wild talk of delirium, sometimes that it may have referred to some band of people, perhaps to these very gipsies in the plantation. I do not know whether the spotted handkerchiefs which so many of them wear over their heads might have suggested the strange adjective which she used."

Holmes shook his head like a man who is far from being satisfied.

"These are very deep waters," said he; "pray go on with your narrative."

"Two years have passed since then, and my life has been until lately lonelier than ever. A month ago, however, a dear friend, whom I have known for many years, has done me the honour to ask my hand in marriage. His name is Armitage—Percy Armitage—the second son of Mr Armitage, of Crane Water, near Reading. My stepfather has offered no opposition to the match, and we are to be married in the course of the spring. Two days ago some repairs were started in the west wing of the building, and my bedroom wall has been pierced, so that I have had to move into the chamber in which my sister died, and to sleep in the very bed in which she slept. Imagine, then, my thrill of terror when last night, as I lay awake, thinking over her terrible fate, I suddenly heard in the silence of the night the low whistle which had been the herald of her own death. I sprang up and lit the lamp, but nothing was to be seen in the room. I was too shaken to go to bed again, however, so I dressed, and as soon as it was daylight I slipped down, got a dog-cart at the Crown Inn, which is opposite, and drove to Leatherhead, from whence I have come on this morning, with the one object of seeing you and asking your advice."

"You have done wisely," said my friend. "But have you told me all?"

"Yes, all."

"Miss Roylott, you have not. You are screening your stepfather."

"Why, what do you mean?"

For answer Holmes pushed back the frill of black lace which fringed the hand that lay upon our visitor's knee. Five little livid spots, the marks of four fingers and a thumb, were printed upon the white wrist.

"You have been cruelly used," said Holmes.

The lady coloured deeply, and covered over her injured wrist. "He is a hard man," she said, "and perhaps he hardly knows his own strength."

There was a long silence, during which Holmes leaned his chin upon his hands and stared into the crackling fire.

"This is a very deep business," he said at last. "There are a thousand details which I should desire to know before I decide upon our course of action. Yet we have not a moment to lose. If we were to come to Stoke Moran today, would it be possible for us to see over these rooms without the knowledge of your step-father?"

"As it happens, he spoke of coming into town today upon some most important business. It is probable that he will be away all day, and that there would be nothing to disturb you. We have a housekeeper, now, but she is old and foolish, and I could easily get her out of the way."

"Excellent. You are not averse to this trip, Watson?"

"By no means."

"Then we shall both come. What are you going to do your-self?"

"I have one or two things which I would wish to do now that I am in town. But I shall return by the twelve o'clock train, so as to be there in time for your coming."

"And you may expect us early in the afternoon. I have myself some small business matters to attend to. Will you not wait and breakfast?"

"No, I must go. My heart is lightened already since I have con-fided my trouble to you. I shall look forward to seeing you again this afternoon."

She dropped her thick black veil over her face, and glided from the room.

"And what do you think of it all, Watson?" asked Sherlock Holmes, leaning back in his chair.

"It seems to me to be a most dark and sinister business."

"Dark enough and sinister enough."

"Yet if the lady is correct in saying that the flooring and walls are sound, and that the door, window, and chimney are impassable, then her sister must have been undoubtedly alone when she met her mysterious end."

"What becomes, then, of these nocturnal whistles, and what of the very peculiar words of the dying woman?"

"I cannot think."

"When you combine the ideas of whistles at night, the presence of a band of gipsies who are on intimate terms with this old doctor, the fact we have every reason to believe that the doctor has an interest in preventing his stepdaughter's marriage, the dying allusion to a band, and finally, the fact that Miss Helen Stoner heard a metallic clang, which might have been caused by one of those metal bars which secured the shutters falling back into their place, I think there is good ground to think that the mystery may be cleared along those lines."

"But what, then, did the gipsies do?"

"I cannot imagine."

"I see many objections to any such a theory."

"And so do I. It is precisely for that reason that we are going to Stoke Moran this day. I want to see whether the objections are fatal, or if they may be explained away. But what, in the name of the devil!"

The ejaculation had been drawn from my companion by the fact that our door had been suddenly dashed open, and that a huge man framed himself in the aperture. His costume was a peculiar mixture of the professional and of the agricultural, having a black top hat, a long frock-coat, and a pair of high gaiters, with a hunting-crop swinging in his hand. So tall was he that his hat actually brushed the cross-bar of the doorway, and his breadth seemed to span it across from side to side. A large face, seared with a thousand wrinkles, burned yellow with the sun, and marked with very evil passion, was turned from one to the other of us, while his deep-set, bile-shot eyes, and the high thin fleshless nose, gave him somewhat the resemblance to a fierce old bird of prey.

"Which of you is Holmes?" asked this apparition.

"My name, sir, but you have the advantage of me," said my companion quietly.

"I am Dr Grimesby Roylott, of Stoke Moran."

"Indeed, Doctor," said Holmes blandly. "Pray take a seat."

"I will do nothing of the kind. My stepdaughter has been here. I have traced her. What has she been saying to you?"

"It is a little cold for this time of the year," said Holmes.

"What has she been saying to you?" screamed the old man furiously.

"But I have heard that the crocuses promise well," continued my companion imperturbably.

"Ha! You put me off, do you?" said our new visitor, taking a step forward and shaking his hunting-crop. "I know you, you scoundrel! I have heard of you before. You are Holmes the meddler."

My friend smiled.

"Holmes the busybody!"

His smile broadened.

"Holmes the Scotland Yard Jack-in-office."

Holmes chuckled heartily. "Your conversation is most entertaining," said he. "When you go out close the door, for there is a decided draught."

"I will go when I have had my say. Don't you dare to meddle with my affairs. I know that Miss Stoner has been here—I traced her! I am a dangerous man to fall foul of! See here." He stepped swiftly forward, seized the poker, and bent it into a curve with his huge brown hands.

"See that you keep yourself out of my grip," he snarled, and hurling the twisted poker into the fire-place, he strode out of the room.

"He seems a very amiable person," said Holmes, laughing. "I am not quite so bulky, but if he had remained I might have shown him that my grip was not much more feeble than his own." As he spoke he picked up the steel poker, and with a sudden effort straightened it out again.

"Fancy his having the insolence to confound me with the official detective force! This incident gives zest to our investigation, however, and I only trust that our little friend will not suffer from her imprudence in allowing this brute to trace her. And now, Watson, we shall order breakfast, and afterwards I shall walk down to Doctors' Commons, where I hope to get some data which may help us in this matter."

It was nearly one o'clock when Sherlock Holmes returned from his excursion. He held in his hand a sheet of blue paper, scrawled over with notes and figures.

"I have seen the will of the deceased wife," said he. "To determine its exact meaning I have been obliged to work out the present prices of the investments with which it is concerned. The total income, which at the time of the wife's death was little short of £ 1,100, is now through the fall in agricultural prices not more than £ 750. Each daughter can claim an income of £ 250, in case of marriage. It is evident, therefore, that if both girls had married this beauty would have had a mere pittance, while even one of them would cripple him to a serious extent. My morning's work has not been wasted, since it has proved that he has the very strongest motives for standing in the way of anything of the sort. And now, Watson, this is too serious for dawdling, especially as the old man is aware that we are interesting ourselves in his affairs, so if you are ready we shall call a cab and drive to Waterloo. I should be very much obliged if you would slip your revolver into your pocket. An Eley's No. 2 is an excellent argument with gentlemen who can twist steel pokers into knots. That and a toothbrush are, I think, all that we need."

At Waterloo we were fortunate in catching a train for Leatherhead, where we hired a trap at the station inn and drove for four or five miles through the lovely Surrey lanes. It was a perfect day, with a bright sun and a few fleecy clouds in the heavens. The trees and wayside hedges were just throwing out their green shoots, and the air was full of the pleasant smell of the moist earth. To me at least there was a strange contrast between the sweet promise of the spring and this sinister quest upon which we were engaged. My companion sat in front of the trap, his arms folded, his hat pulled down over his eyes, and his chin sunk upon his breast, buried in the deepest thought. Suddenly, however, he started, tapped me on the shoulder, and pointed over the meadows.

"Look there!" said he.

A heavily-timbered park stretched up in a gentle slope, thickening into a grove at the highest point. From admidst the branches there jutted out the grey gables and high roof-tree of a very old mansion.

"Stoke Moran?" said he.

"Yes, sir, that be the house of Dr Grimesby Roylott," remarked the driver.

"There is some building going on over there," said Holmes; "that is where we are going."

"There's the village," said the driver, pointing to a cluster of roofs some distance to the left; "but if you want to get to the house, you'll find it shorter to go over this stile, and so by the foot-path over the fields. There it is, where the lady is walking."

"And the lady, I fancy, is Miss Stoner," observed Holmes, shading his eyes. "Yes, I think we had better do as you suggest."

We got off, paid our fare, and the trap rattled back on its way to Leatherhead.

"I thought it as well," said Holmes, as we climbed the stile, "that this fellow should think we had come here as architects, or on some definite business. It may stop his gossip. Good afternoon, Miss Stoner, You see that we have been as good as our word."

Our client of the morning had hurried forward to meet us with a face which spoke her joy. "I have been waiting so eagerly for you," she cried, shaking hands with us warmly. "All has turned out splendidly. Dr Roylott has gone to town, and it is unlikely that he will be back before evening."

155

"We have had the pleasure of making the Doctor's acquaintance," said Holmes, and in a few words he sketched out what had occurred. Miss Stoner turned white to the lips as she listened.

"Good Heavens!" she cried, "he has followed me, then."

"So it appears."

"He is so cunning that I never know when I am safe from him. What will he say when he returns?"

"He must guard himself, for he may find that there is someone more cunning than himself upon his track. You must lock yourself from him tonight. If he is violent, we shall take you away to your aunt's at Harrow. Now, we must make the best use of our time, so kindly take us at once to the rooms which we are to examine."

The building was of grey, lichen-blotched stone, with a high central portion, and two curving wings, like the claws of a crab, thrown out on each side. In one of these wings the windows were broken, and blocked with wooden boards, while the roof was partly caved in, a picture of ruin. The central portion was in little better repair, but the righthand block was comparatively modern, and the blinds in the windows, with the blue smoke curling up from the chimneys, showed that this was where the family resided. Some scaffolding had been erected against the end wall, and the stonework had been broken into, but there were no signs of any workmen at the moment of our visit. Holmes walked slowly up and down the ill-trimmed lawn, and examined with deep attention the outside of the windows.

"This, I take it, belongs to the room in which you used to sleep, the centre one to your sister's, and the one next to the main building to Dr Roylott's chamber?"

"Exactly so. But I am now sleeping in the middle one."

"Pending the alterations, as I understand. By the way, there does not seem to be any very pressing need for repairs at that end wall."

"There were none. I believe that it was an excuse to move me from my room."

"Ah! that is suggestive. Now, on the other side of this narrow wing runs the corridor from which these three rooms open. There are windows in it, of course?"

"Yes, but very small ones. Too narrow for anyone to pass through."

"As you both locked your doors at night your rooms were unapproachable from that side. Now, would you have the kindness to go into your room, and to bar your shutters."

Miss Stoner did so, and Holmes, after a careful examination through the open window, endeavoured in every way to force the shutter open, but without success. There was no slit through which a knife could be passed to raise the bar. Then with his lens he tested the hinges, but they were of solid iron, built firmly into the massive masonry. "Hum!" said he, scratching his chin in some perplexity, "my theory certainly presents some difficulties. No one could pass these shutters if they were bolted. Well, we shall see if the inside throws any light upon the matter."

A small side-door led into the whitewashed corridor from which the three bedrooms opened. Holmes refused to examine the third chamber, so we passed at once to the second, that in which Miss Stoner was now sleeping, and in which her sister had met her fate. It was a homely little room, with a low ceiling and a gaping fireplace, after the fashion of old country houses. A brown chest of drawers stood in one corner, a narrow white counterpaned bed in another, and a dressing-table on the left-hand side of the window. These articles, with two small wickerwork chairs, made up all the furniture in the room, save for a square of Wilton carpet in the centre. The boards round and the panelling of the walls were brown, worm-eaten oak, so old and discoloured that it may have dated from the original building of the house. Holmes drew one of the chairs into a corner and sat silent, while his eyes travelled round and round and up and down, taking in every detail of the apartment.

"Where does that bell communicate with?" he asked at last, pointing to a thick bell-rope which hung down beside the bed, the tassel actually lying upon the pillow.

"He threw himself down upon his face with his lens in his hand . . ."

"It goes to the housekeeper's room."

"It looks newer than the other things?"

"Yes, it was only put there a couple of years ago."

"Your sister asked for it, I suppose?"

"No, I never heard of her using it. We used always to get what we wanted for ourselves."

"Indeed, it seemed unnecessary to put so nice a bell-pull there. You will excuse me for a few minutes while I satisfy myself as to this floor." He threw himself down upon his face with his lens in his hand, and crawled swiftly backwards and forwards, examining minutely the cracks between the boards. Then he did the same with the woodwork with which the chamber was panelled. Finally he walked over to the bed and spent some time in staring at it, and running his eye up and down the wall. Finally he took the bell-rope in his hand and gave it a brisk tug.

"Why, it's a dummy," said he.

"Won't it ring?"

"No, it is not even attached to a wire. This is very interesting. You can see now that it is fastened to a hook just above where the little opening of the ventilator is."

"How very absurd! I never noticed that before."

"Very strange!" muttered Holmes, pulling at the rope. "There are one or two very singular points about this room. For example, what a fool a builder must be to open a ventilator in another room, when, with the same trouble, he might have communicated with the outside air!"

"That is also quite modern," said the lady.

"Done about the same time as the bell-rope," remarked Holmes.

"Yes, there were several little changes carried out about that time."

"They seem to have been of a most interesting character—dummy bellropes, and ventilators which do not ventilate. With your permission, Miss Stoner, we shall now carry our researches into the inner apartment."

Dr Grimesby Roylott's chamber was larger than that of his

stepdaughter, but was plainly furnished. A camp bed, a small wooden shelf full of books, mostly of a technical character, an arm-chair beside the bed, a plain wooden chair against the wall, a round table, and a large iron safe were the principal things which met the eye. Holmes walked slowly round and examined each and all of them with the keenest interest.

"What's in here?" he asked, tapping the safe.

"My stepfather's business papers."

"Oh! you have seen inside, then?"

"Only once, some years ago. I remember that it was full of papers."

"There isn't a cat in it, for example?"

"No. What a strange idea!"

"Well, look at this!" He took up a small saucer of milk which stood on the top of it.

"No; we don't keep a cat. But there is a cheetah and a baboon."

"Ah, yes, of course! Well, a cheetah is just a big cat, and yet a saucer of milk does not go very far in satisfying its wants, I dare say. There is one point which I should wish to determine." He squatted down in front of the wooden chair, and examined the seat of it with the greatest attention.

"Thank you. That is quite settled," said he, rising and putting his lens in his pocket. "Hullo! here is something interesting!"

The object which had caught his eye was a small dog-lash hung on one corner of the bed. The lash, however, was curled upon itself, and tied so as to make a loop of whipcord.

"What do you make of that, Watson?"

"It's a common enough lash, but I don't know why it should be tied."

"That is not quite so common, is it? Ah, me! it's a wicked world, and when a clever man turns his brain to crime it is the worst of all. I think that I have seen enough now, Miss Stoner, and, with your permission, we shall walk out upon the lawn."

I had never seen my friend's face so grim, or his brow so dark, as it was when we turned from the scene of this investigation. We had walked several times up and down the lawn, neither

Miss Stoner nor myself liking to break in upon his thoughts before he roused himself from his reverie.

"It is very essential, Miss Stoner," said he, "that you should absolutely follow my advice in every respect."

"I shall most certainly do so."

"The matter is too serious for any hesitation. Your life may depend upon your compliance."

"I assure you that I am in your hands."

"In the first place, both my friend and I must spend the night in your room."

Both Miss Stoner and I gazed at him in astonishment.

"Yes, it must be so. Let me explain. I believe that that is the village inn over there?"

"Yes, that is the 'Crown'."

"Very good. Your windows would be visible from there?"

"Certainly."

"You must confine yourself to your room, on pretence of a headache, when your stepfather comes back. Then when you hear him retire for the night, you must open the shutters of your window, undo the hasp, put your lamp there as a signal to us, and then withdraw with everything which you are likely to want into the room which you used to occupy. I have no doubt that, in spite of the repairs, you could manage there for one night."

"Oh, yes, easily."

"The rest you will leave in our hands."

"But what will you do?"

"We shall spend the night in your room, and we shall investigate the cause of this noise which has disturbed you."

"I believe, Mr Holmes, that you have already made up your mind," said Miss Stoner, laying her hand upon my companion's sleeve.

"Perhaps I have."

"Then for pity's sake tell me what was the cause of my sister's death."

"I should prefer to have clearer proofs before I speak."

"You can at least tell me whether my own thought is correct, and if she died from sudden fright."

"No, I do not think so. I think that there was probably some more tangible cause. And now, Miss Stoner, we must leave you, for if Dr Roylott returned and saw us, our journey would be in vain. Goodbye, and be brave, for if you will do what I have told you, you may rest assured that we shall soon drive away the dangers that threaten you."

Sherlock Holmes and I had no difficulty in engaging a bedroom and sitting-room at the Crown Inn. They were on the upper floor, and from our window we could command a view of the avenue gate, and of the inhabited wing of Stoke Moran Manor House. At dusk we saw Dr Grimesby Roylott drive past, his huge form looming up beside the little figure of the lad who drove him. The boy had some slight difficulty in undoing the heavy iron gates, and we heard the hoarse roar of the Doctor's voice, and saw the fury with which he shook his clenched fists at him. The trap drove on, and a few minutes later we saw a sudden light spring up among the trees as the lamp was lit in one of the sitting-rooms.

"Do you know, Watson," said Holmes, as we sat together in the gathering darkness. "I have really some scruples as to taking you tonight. There is a distinct element of danger."

"Can I be of assistance?"

"Your presence might be invaluable."

"Then I shall certainly come."

"It is very kind of you."

"You speak of danger. You have evidently seen more in these rooms than was visible to me."

"No, but I fancy that I may have deduced a little more. I imagine that you saw all that I did."

"I saw nothing remarkable save the bell-rope, and what purpose that could answer I confess is more than I can imagine."

"You saw the ventilator, too?"

"Yes, but I do not think that it is a very unusual thing to have a small opening between two rooms. It was so small that a rat could hardly pass through."

"I knew that we should find a ventilator before ever we came to Stoke Moran."

"My dear Holmes!"

"Oh, yes, I did. You remember in her statement Miss Stoner said that her sister could smell Dr Roylott's cigar. Now, of course that suggests at once that there must be a communication between the two rooms. It could only be a small one, or it would have been remarked upon at the coroner's inquiry. I deduced a ventilator."

"But what harm can there be in that?"

"Well, there is at least a curious coincidence of dates. A ventilator is made, a cord is hung, and a lady who sleeps in the bed dies. Does that not strike you?"

"I cannot as yet see any connection."

"Did you observe anything very peculiar about that bed?"

"No."

"It was clamped to the floor. Did you ever see a bed fastened like that before?"

"I cannot say that I have."

"The lady could not move her bed. It must always be in the same relative position to the ventilator and to the rope—for so we may call it, since it was clearly never meant for a bell-pull."

"Holmes," I cried, "I seem to see dimly what you are hinting at. We are only just in time to prevent some subtle and horrible crime."

"Subtle enough and horrible enough. When a doctor does go wrong he is the first of criminals. He has nerve and he has knowledge. Palmer and Pritchard were among the heads of their profession. This man strikes even deeper, but I think Watson, that we shall be able to strike even deeper still. But we shall have horrors enough before the night is over: for goodness' sake let us have a quiet pipe, and turn our minds for a few hours to something more cheerful."

163

About nine o'clock the light among the trees was extinguished, and all was dark in the direction of the Manor House. Two hours passed slowly away, and then, suddenly, just at the stroke of eleven, a single bright light shone out right in front of us.

"That is our signal," said Holmes, springing to his feet; "it comes from the middle window."

As we passed out he exchanged a few words with the landlord, explaining that we were going on a late visit to an acquaintance, and that it was possible that we might spend the night there. A moment later we were out on the dark road, a chill wind blowing in our faces, and one yellow light twinkling in front of us through the gloom to guide us on our sombre errand.

There was little difficulty in entering the grounds, for unrepaired breaches gaped in the old park wall. Making our way among the trees, we reached the lawn, crossed it, and were about to enter through the window, when out from a clump of laurel bushes there darted what seemed to be a hideous and distorted child, who threw itself on the grass with writhing limbs, and then ran swiftly across the lawn into the darkness.

"My God!" I whispered, "did you see it?"

Holmes was for a minute as startled as I. His hand closed like a vice upon my wrist in his agitation. Then he broke into a low laugh, and put his lips to my ear.

"It is a nice household," he murmured; "that is the baboon."

I had forgotten the strange pets which the Doctor affected. There was a cheetah, too; perhaps we might find it upon our shoulders at any moment. I confess that I felt easier in my mind when, after following Holmes' example and slipping off my shoes, I found myself inside the bedroom. My companion noiselessly closed the shutters, moved the lamp on to the table, and cast his eyes round the room. All was as we had seen it in the day time. Then creeping up to me and making a trumpet of his hand, he whispered into my ear again so gently that it was all I could do to distinguish the words:

"The least sound would be fatal to our plans."

I nodded to show that I had heard.

164

"We must sit without a light. He would see it through the ventilator."

I nodded again.

"Do not go to sleep; your very life may depend upon it. Have your pistol ready in case we should need it. I will sit on the side of the bed, and you in the chair."

I took out my revolver and laid it on the corner of the table.

Holmes had brought up a long thin cane, and this he placed upon the bed beside him. By it he laid the box of matches and the stump of a candle. Then he turned down the lamp and we were left in darkness.

How shall I ever forget that dreadful vigil? I could not hear a sound, not even the drawing of a breath, and yet I knew that my companion sat open-eyed, within a few feet of me in the same state of nervous tension in which I was myself. The shutters cut off the least ray of light, and we waited in absolute darkness. From outside came the occasional cry of a night-bird, and once at our very window a long-drawn cat-like whine, which told us that the cheetah was indeed at liberty. Far away we could hear the deep tones of the parish clock, which boomed out every quarter of an hour. How long they seemed, those quarters! Twelve o'clock, and one, and two, and three, and still we sat waiting silently for whatever might befall.

Suddenly there was the momentary gleam of a light up in the direction of the ventilator, which vanished immediately, but was succeeded by a strong smell of burning oil and heated metal. Someone in the next room had lit a dark lantern. I heard a gentle sound of movement, and then all was silent, once more, though the smell grew stronger. For half an hour I sat with straining ears. Then suddenly another sound became audible—a very gentle, soothing sound, like that of a small jet of steam escaping continually from a kettle. The instant that we heard it, Holmes sprang from the bed, struck a match, and lashed furiously with his cane at the bell-pull.

"You see it, Watson?" he yelled. "You see it?"

But I saw nothing. At the moment when Holmes struck the

light I heard a low, clear whistle, but the sudden glare flashing into my weary eyes made it impossible for me to tell what it was at which my friend lashed so savagely. I could, however, see that his face was deadly pale, and filled with horror and loathing.

He had ceased to strike, and was gazing up at the ventilator, when suddenly there broke from the silence of the night the most horrible cry to which I have ever listened. It swelled up louder and louder, a hoarse yell of pain and fear and anger all mingled in the one dreadful shriek. They say that away down in the village, and even in the distant parsonage, that cry raised the sleepers from their beds. It struck cold to our hearts, and I stood gazing at Holmes, and he at me, until the last echoes of it had died away into the silence from which it rose.

"What can it mean?" I gasped.

"It means that it is all over," Holmes answered. "And perhaps, after all, it is for the best. Take your pistol, and we shall enter Dr Roylott's room."

With a grave face he lit the lamp, and led the way down the corridor. Twice he struck at the chamber door without any reply from within. Then he turned the handle and entered, I at his heels, with the cocked pistol in my hand.

It was a singular sight which met our eyes. On the table stood a dark lantern with the shutter half open, throwing a brilliant beam of light upon the iron safe, the door of which was ajar. Beside this table, on the wooden chair, sat Dr Grimesby Roylott, clad in a long grey dressing-gown, his bare ankles protruding beneath, and his feet thrust into red heel-less Turkish slippers. Across his lap lay the short stock with the long lash which we had noticed during the day. His chin was cocked upwards, and his eyes were fixed in a dreadful rigid stare at the corner of the ceiling. Round his brow he had a peculiar yellow band, with brownish speckles, which seemed to be bound tightly round his head. As we entered he made neither sound nor motion.

"The band! The speckled band!" whispered Holmes.

166

"*In an instant his strange headgear began to move...*"

I took a step forward. In an instant his strange headgear began to move, and there reared itself from among his hair the squat diamond-shaped head and puffed neck of a loathsome serpent.

"It is a swamp adder!" cried Holmes—"the deadliest snake in India. He has died within ten seconds of being bitten. Violence does, in truth, recoil upon the violent, and the schemer falls into the pit which he digs for another. Let us thrust this creature back into its den, and we can then remove Miss Stoner to some place of shelter, and let the county police know what has happened."

As he spoke he drew the dog whip swiftly from the dead man's lap, and throwing the noose round the reptile's neck, he drew it from its horrid perch, and, carrying it at arm's length, threw it into the iron safe, which he closed upon it.

Such are the true facts of the death of Dr Grimesby Roylott, of Stoke Moran. It is not necessary that I should prolong a narrative which has already run to too great a length, by telling how we broke the sad news to the terrified girl, how we conveyed her by the morning train to the care of her good aunt at Harrow, of how the slow process of official inquiry came to the conclusion that the Doctor met his fate while indiscreetly playing with a dangerous pet. The little which I had yet to learn of the case was told me by Sherlock Holmes as we travelled back next day.

"I had," said he, "come to an entirely erroneous conclusion which shows, my dear Watson, how dangerous it always is to reason from insufficient data. The presence of the gipsies, and the use of the word 'band', which was used by the poor girl, no doubt, to explain the appearance which she had caught a horrid glimpse of by the light of her match, were sufficient to put me upon an entirely wrong scent. I can only claim the merit that I instantly reconsidered my position when, however, it became clear to me that whatever danger threatened an occupant of the room could not come either from the window or the door. My attention was speedily drawn, as I have already remarked to you, to this ventilator, and to the bell-rope which hung down to the bed. The discovery that this was a dummy, and that the bed was clamped to the floor, instantly gave rise to the suspicion that the rope was there as a bridge for something passing through the hole, and coming to the bed. The idea of a snake instantly occurred to me, and when I coupled it with my knowledge that the Doctor was furnished with a supply of creatures from India, I felt that I was probably on the right track. The idea of using a form of poison which could not possibly be discovered by any chemical test was just such a one as would occur to a clever and ruthless man who had had an Eastern training. The rapidity with which such a poison would take effect would also, from his point of view, be an advantage. It would be a sharp-eyed coroner indeed who could distinguish the two little dark punctures which would show where the poison fangs had done their work. Then I thought of the whistle. Of course, he must recall the snake before the morning light revealed it to the victim. He had trained it, probably by the use of the milk which we saw, to return to him when summoned. He would put it through the ventilator at the hour that he thought best, with the certainty that it would crawl down the rope, and land on the bed. It might or might not bite the occupant, perhaps she might escape every night for a week, but sooner or later she must fall a victim.

"I had come to these conclusions before ever I had entered his room. An inspection cf his chair showed me that he had been in the habit of standing on it, which of course would be necessary in order that he should reach the ventilator. The sight of the safe, the saucer of milk, and the loop of whipcord were enough to finally dispel any doubts which may have remained. The metallic clang heard by Miss Stoner was obviously caused by her stepfather hastily closing the door of his safe upon its terrible occupant. Having once made up my mind, you know the steps which I took in order to put the matter to the proof. I heard the creature hiss, as I have no doubt that you did also, and I instantly lit the light and attacked it."

"With the result of driving it through the ventilator."

"And also with the result of causing it to turn upon its master at the other side. Some of the blows of my cane came home, and roused its snakish temper, so that it flew upon the first person it saw. In this way I am no doubt indirectly responsible for Dr Grimesby Roylott's death, and I cannot say that it is likely to weigh very heavily upon my conscience."

The Clinging Death

BY JACK LONDON

White Fang was the cub of a wolf father and half-wolf, half-dog mother. He is stopped from being completely wild when he is taken into an Indian camp. He is trained to pull a dog sledge and becomes leader of the dogs. Through his superb skills as a fighter, White Fang becomes the property of Beauty Smith. Goaded into wild ferocity by his cruel master, White Fang becomes the fiercest fighting dog ever seen in the Yukon. He is called the "Fighting Wolf" and he even defeats a lynx. Eventually no dog can be found to fight him until one spring, Tim Keenan brings the first bull-dog ever seen in the Klondyke...

Beauty Smith slipped the chain from his neck and stepped back.

For once White Fang did not make an immediate attack. He stood still, ears pricked forward, alert and curious, surveying the strange animal that faced him. He had never seen such a dog before. Tim Keenan shoved the bull-dog forward with a muttered "Go to it". The animal waddled toward the centre of the circle, short and squat and ungainly. He came to a stop and blinked across at White Fang.

There were cries from the crowd of "Go to him, Cherokee! Sick 'm, Cherokee! Eat 'm up!"

But Cherokee did not seem anxious to fight. He turned his

171

head and blinked at the men who shouted, at the same time wagging his stump of a tail good-naturedly. He was not afraid, but merely lazy. Besides, it did not seem to him that it was intended he should fight with the dog he saw before him. He was not used to fighting with that kind of dog, and he was waiting for them to bring on the real dog.

Tim Keenan stepped in and bent over Cherokee, fondling him on both sides of the shoulders with hands that rubbed against the grain of the hair and that made slight, pushing-forward movements. These were so many suggestions. Also, their effect was irritating, for Cherokee began to growl, very softly, deep down in his throat. There was a correspondence in rhythm between the growls and the movements of the man's hands. The growls rose in the throat with the culmination of each forward-pushing movement, and ebbed down to start up afresh with the beginning of the next movement. The end of each movement was the accent of the rhythm, the movement ending abruptly and the growling rising with a jerk.

This was not without its effect on White Fang. The hair began to rise on his neck and across the shoulders. Tim Keenan gave a final shove forward and stepped back again. As the impetus that carried Cherokee forward died down, he continued to go forward of his own volition, in a swift, bow-legged run. Then White Fang struck. A cry of startled admiration went up. He had covered the distance and gone in more like a cat than a dog; and with the same cat-like swiftness he had slashed with his fangs and leaped clear.

The bull-dog was bleeding at the back of one ear from a rip in his thick neck. He gave no sign, did not even snarl, but turned and followed after White Fang. The display on both sides, the quickness of the one and the steadiness of the other, had excited the partisan spirit of the crowd, and the men were making new bets and increasing original bets. Again and yet again White Fang sprang in, slashed, and got away untouched; and still his strange foe followed after him, without too great haste, not slowly, but deliberately and determinedly, in a businesslike sort of way. There was purpose in his method — something for him to do that he was intent upon doing and from which nothing could distract him.

His whole demeanour, every action, was stamped with this purpose. It puzzled White Fang. Never had he seen such a dog. It had no hair protection. It was soft, and bled easily. There was no thick mat of fur to baffle White Fang's teeth as they were often baffled by dogs of his own breed. Each time that his teeth struck they sank easily into the yielding flesh, while the animal did not seem able to defend itself. Another disconcerting thing was that it made no outcry, such as he had been accustomed to with the other dogs he had fought. Beyond a growl or a grunt, the dog took its punishment silently. And never did it flag in its pursuit of him.

Not that Cherokee was slow. He could turn and whirl swiftly enough, but White Fang was never there. Cherokee was puzzled too. He had never fought before with a dog with which he could not close. The desire to close had always been mutual. But here was a dog that kept at a distance, dancing and dodging here and there and all about. And when it did get its teeth into him, it did not hold on, but let go instantly and darted away again.

But White Fang could not get at the soft underside of the throat. The bull-dog stood too short, while its massive jaws were an added protection, White Fang darted in and out unscathed, while Cherokee's wounds increased. Both sides of his neck and head were ripped and slashed. He bled freely, but showed no signs of being disconcerted. He continued his plodding pursuit, though once, for the moment baffled, he came to a full stop and blinked at the men who looked on, at the same time wagging his stump of a tail as an expression of his willingness to fight.

In that moment White Fang was in upon him and out, in passing ripping his trimmed remnant of an ear. With a slight manifestation of anger, Cherokee took up the pursuit again, running on the inside of the circle White Fang was making, and striving to fasten his deadly grip on White Fang's throat. The bull-dog missed by a hair's-breadth, and cries of praise went up as White Fang doubled suddenly out of danger in the opposite direction.

The time went by. White Fang still danced on, dodging and doubling, leaping in and out, and ever inflicting damage. And still the bull-dog, with grim certitude, toiled after him. Sooner or later he would accomplish his purpose, get the grip that would win the battle. In the meantime, he accepted all the punishment the other could deal him. His tufts of ears had become tassels, his neck and shoulders were slashed in a score of pieces, and his very lips were cut and bleeding — all from those lightning snaps that were beyond his foreseeing and guarding.

Time and again White Fang had attempted to knock Cherokee off his feet; but the difference in their height was too great. Cherokee was too squat, too close to the ground. White Fang tried the trick once too often. The chance came in one of his quick doublings and countercirclings. He caught Cherokee with head turned away as he whirled more slowly. His shoulder was exposed. White Fang drove in upon it; but his own shoulder was high above, while he struck with such force that his momentum carried him on across over the other's body. For the first time in his fighting history, men saw White Fang lose his footing. His body turned a half-somersault in the air, and he would have landed on his back had he not twisted, catlike, still in the air, in the effort to bring his feet to the earth. As it was, he struck heavily on his side. The next instant he was on his feet, but in that instant Cherokee's teeth closed on his throat.

It was not a good grip, being too low down toward the chest; but Cherokee held on. White Fang sprang to his feet and tore wildly around, trying to shake off the bull-dog's body. It made him frantic, this clinging dragging weight. It bound his movements, restricted his freedom. It was like the trap, and all his instinct resented it and revolted against it. It was a mad revolt. For several minutes he was to all intents insane. The basic life that was in him took charge of him. The will to exist of his body surged over him. He was dominated by this mere flesh-love of life. All intelligence was gone. It was as though he had no brain. His reason

174

"*White Fang sprang to his feet and tore wildly around trying to shake off the bulldog's grip.*"

was unseated by the blind yearning of the flesh to exist and move, at all hazards to move, to continue to move, for movement was the expression of its existence.

Round and round he went, whirling and turning and reversing, trying to shake off the fifty-pound weight that dragged at his throat. The bull-dog did little but keep his grip. Sometimes, and rarely, he managed to get his feet to the earth and for a moment to brace himself against White Fang. But the next moment his footing would be lost, and he would be dragging around in the whirl of one of White Fang's mad gyrations. Cherokee identified himself with his instinct. He knew that he was doing the right thing by holding on, and there came to him certain blissful thrills of satisfaction. At such moments he even closed his eyes and allowed his body to be hurled hither and thither, willy-nilly, careless of any hurt that might thereby come to it. That did not count. The grip was the thing, and the grip he kept.

White Fang ceased only when he had tired himself out. He could do nothing, and he could not understand. Never, in all his fighting, had this thing happened. The dogs he had fought with did not fight that way. With them it was snap and slash and get away, snap and slash and get away. He lay partly on his side, panting for breath. Cherokee still holding his grip, urged against him, trying to get him over entirely on his side. White Fang resisted, and he could feel the jaws shifting their grip, slightly relaxing and coming together again in a chewing movement. Each shift brought the grip closer in to his throat. The bull-dog's method was to hold what he had, and when opportunity favoured, to work in for more. Opportunity favoured when White Fang remained quiet. When White Fang struggled, Cherokee was content merely to hold on.

The bulging back of Cherokee's neck was the only portion of his body that White Fang's teeth could reach. He got hold toward the base, where the neck comes out from the shoulders; but he did not know the chewing method of fighting, nor were his jaws adapted to it. He spasmodically ripped and tore with his fangs for a space. Then a change in their position diverted him. The

176

bull-dog had managed to roll him over on his back, and still hanging on to his throat, was on top of him. Like a cat, White Fang bowed his hind-quarters in, and, with the feet digging into his enemy's abdomen above him, he began to claw with long tearing strokes. Cherokee might well have been disembowelled had he not quickly pivoted on his grip and got his body off of White Fang's and at right angles to it.

There was no escaping that grip. It was like Fate itself, and as inexorable. Slowly it shifted up along the jugular. All that saved White Fang from death was the loose skin of his neck and the thick fur that covered it. This served to form a large roll in Cherokee's mouth, the fur of which well-nigh defied his teeth. But bit by bit, whenever the chance offered, he was getting more of the loose skin and fur in his mouth. The result was that he was slowly throttling White Fang. The latter's breath was drawn with greater and greater difficulty as the moments went by.

It began to look as though the battle was over. The backers of Cherokee waxed jubilant and offered ridiculous odds. White Fang's backers were correspondingly depressed, and refused bets of ten to one and twenty to one, though one man was rash enough to close a wager of fifty to one. This man was Beauty Smith. He took a step into the ring and pointed his finger at White Fang. Then he began to laugh derisively and scornfully. This produced the desired effect. White Fang went wild with rage. He called up his reserves of strength and gained his feet. As he struggled around the ring, the fifty pounds of his foe ever dragging on his throat, his anger passed on into panic. The basic life of him dominated him again, and his intelligence fled before the will of his flesh to live. Round and round and back again, stumbling and falling and rising, even uprearing at times on his hind-legs and lifting his foe clear of the earth, he struggled vainly to shake off the clinging death.

At last he fell, toppling backward, exhausted; and the bull-dog promptly shifted his grip, getting in closer, mangling more and more of the furfolded flesh, throttling White Fang more severely than ever. Shouts of applause went up for the victor, and there were many cries of "Cherokee!" "Cherokee!" To this Cherokee responded by vigorous wagging of the stump of his tail. But the clamour of approval did not distract him. There was no sympathetic relation between his tail and his massive jaws. The one might wag, but the others held their terrible grip on White Fang's throat.

It was at this time that a diversion came to the spectators. There was a jingle of bells. Dog-mushers' cries were heard. Everybody, save Beauty Smith, looked apprehensively, the fear of the police strong upon them. But they saw, up the trail and not down, two men running with sled and dogs. They were evidently coming down the creek from some prospecting trip. At sight of the crowd they stopped their dogs and came over and joined it, curious to see the cause of the excitement. The dog-musher wore a moustache, but the other, a taller and younger man, was smooth-shaven, his skin rosy from the pounding of his blood and the running in the frosty air.

White Fang had practically ceased struggling. Now and again he resisted spasmodically and to no purpose. He could get little air, and that little grew less and less under the merciless grip that ever tightened. In spite of his armour of fur, the great vein of his throat would have long since been torn open, had not the first grip of the bull-dog been so low down as to be practically on the chest. It had taken Cherokee a long time to shift that grip upward, and this had also tended further to clog his jaws with fur and skin-fold.

In the meantime, the abysmal brute in Beauty Smith had been rising up into his brain and mastering the small bit of sanity that he possessed at best. When he saw White Fang's eyes beginning to glaze, he knew beyond doubt that the fight was lost. Then he broke loose. He sprang upon White Fang and began savagely to kick him. There were hisses from the crowd and cries of protest, but that was all. While this went on, and Beauty Smith continued to kick White Fang, there was a commotion in the crowd. The tall young newcomer was forcing his way through, shouldering men right and left without ceremony or gentleness. When he broke

"*At that moment the newcomer's fist landed a smashing blow full in his face.*"

through into the ring, Beauty Smith was just in the act of delivering another kick. All his weight was on one foot, and he was in a state of unstable equilibrium. At that moment the newcomer's fist landed a smashing blow full in his face. Beauty Smith's remaining leg left the ground, and his whole body seemed to lift into the air as he turned over backward and struck the snow. The newcomer turned upon the crowd.

"You cowards!" he cried. "You beasts!"

He was in a rage himself — a sane rage. His grey eyes seemed metallic and steel-like as they flashed upon the crowd. Beauty Smith regained his feet and came toward him, sniffing and cowardly. The newcomer did not understand. He did not know how abject a coward the other was, and thought he was coming back intent on fighting. So, with a "You beast!" he smashed Beauty Smith over backward with a second blow in the face. Beauty Smith decided that the snow was the safest place for him, and lay where he had fallen, making no effort to get up.

"Come on, Matt; lend a hand," the newcomer called to the dog-musher, who had followed him into the ring.

Both men bent over the dogs. Matt took hold of White Fang, ready to pull when Cherokee's jaws should be loosened. This the younger man endeavoured to accomplish by clutching the bulldog's jaws in his hands and trying to spread them. It was a vain undertaking. As he pulled and tugged and wrenched, he kept exclaiming with every expulsion of breath, "Beasts!"

The crowd began to grow unruly, and some of the men were protesting against the spoiling of the sport; but they were silenced when the newcomer lifted his head from his work for a moment and glared at them.

"You damn beasts!" he finally exploded, and went back to his task.

"It's no use, Mr Scott; you can't break'm apart that way," Matt said at last.

The pair paused and surveyed the locked dogs.

"Ain't bleedin' much," Matt announced. "Ain't got all the way in yet."

180

"But he's liable to any moment," Scott answered. "There! Did you see that? He shifted his grip in a bit."

The younger man's excitement and apprehension for White Fang was growing. He struck Cherokee about the head savagely again and again. But that did not loosen the jaws. Cherokee wagged the stump of his tail in advertisement that he understood the meaning of the blows, but that he knew he was himself in the right and only doing his duty by keeping his grip.

"Won't some of you help?" Scott cried desperately at the crowd.

But no help was offered. Instead, the crowd began sarcastically to cheer him on and showered him with facetious advice.

"You'll have to get a pry," Matt counselled.

The other reached into the holster at his hip, drew his revolver, and tried to thrust its muzzle between the bull-dog's jaws. He shoved, and shoved hard, till the grating of the steel against the locked teeth could be distinctly heard. Both men were on their knees, bending over the dogs. Tim Keenan strode into the ring. He paused beside Scott and touched him on the shoulder, saying ominously:

"Don't break them teeth, stranger."

"Then I'll break his neck," Scott retorted, continuing his shoving and wedging with the revolver muzzle.

"I said don't break them teeth," the faro-dealer repeated more ominously than before.

But if it was bluff he intended, it did not work. Scott never desisted from his efforts, though he looked up coolly and asked:

"Your dog?"

The faro-dealer grunted.

"Then get in here and break this grip."

"Well, stranger," the other drawled irritatingly, "I don't mind telling you that's something I ain't worked out for myself. I don't know how to turn the trick."

"Then get out of the way," was the reply, "and don't bother me. I'm busy."

Tim Keenan continued standing over him, but Scott took no further notice of his presence. He had managed to get the muzzle in between the jaws on one side, and was trying to get it out between the jaws on the other side. This accomplished, he pried gently and carefully, loosening the jaws a bit at a time; while Matt, a bit at a time, extricated White Fang's mangled neck.

"Stand by to receive your dog," was Scott's peremptory order to Cherokee's owner.

The faro-dealer stooped down obediently and got a firm hold on Cherokee.

"Now!" Scott warned, giving the final pry.

The dogs were drawn apart, the bull-dog struggling vigorously.

"Take him away," Scott commanded; and Tim Keenan dragged Cherokee back into the crowd.

White Fang made several ineffectual efforts to get up. Once he gained his feet, but his legs were too weak to sustain him, and he slowly wilted and sank back into the snow. His eyes were half closed, and the surface of them was glassy. His jaws were apart, and through them the tongue protruded, draggled and limp. To all appearances he looked like a dog that had been strangled to death. Matt examined him.

"Just about all in," he announced; "but he's breathin' all right."